# I, Lars Hård

Translated, with
an Introduction
and Notes, by
Robert E. Bjork

# I,
# Lars
# Hård

Jan Fridegård

University of Nebraska Press
Lincoln and London

Publication of this
book was aided by a
grant from the Andrew
W. Mellon Foundation.

The paper in this book meets
the guidelines for
permanence and durability
of the Committee on
Production Guidelines for
Book Longevity of the
Council on Library Resources.

Library of Congress Cataloging
in Publication Data

Fridegård, Jan, 1897-1968.
I, Lars Hård.

Translation of: Jag Lars Hård.
I. Bjork, Robert E.,
1949-   .   II. Title.
PT9875.F788J313   1983
839.7'372   83-1098
ISBN 0-8032-1963-6

# Contents

# Acknowledgments

Many have helped move this translation towards publication, and I would like to thank
them briefly here. Dr. Carol P. Hartzog of
UCLA—and of my home—devotedly and
skillfully scrutinized each draft of the entire
book, saving me from innumerable errors, unhappy phrases, and unhappy hours, and Ms.
Aase Fridegård, Jan Fridegård's daughter,
graciously supported my work from my first
translations of her father's short stories to the
final stages of work on this novel. Mr. Sture
Rådström of the Harvard School in Los An-
geles read the first typescript and answered a
number of questions about Fridegård's lan-
guage, while Professor Torborg Lundell of the
University of California at Santa Barbara carefully and expertly examined the penultimate
draft of the translation, offering a number of
suggestions for its improvement. The work of
all these people has made this book a much
better thing. Finally, I would like to thank both
Professor Michael Heim of UCLA for intro-
ducing me to the complexities, frustrations, and
rewards of literary translation, and the *Sverige-
Amerika stiftelse* in Stockholm for giving me a
grant in 1974–75, when my interest in Fridegård first took root.

R. E. B

# Introduction

Jan Fridegård (d. 1968) was born June 14, 1897, into a poor work-ing-class family of seven in Enköpings-Näs, an area in central Sweden just north of Lake Mälar. His father was a *statare* (pro-nounced "stă-tă-rĕ"), a farm laborer tied to a large estate and earn-ing his wages partly in cash but mostly in kind (*stat*). The brutal statare system, which arose in the eighteenth century to support the aristocratic estates and survived until 1945, almost guaranteed illiteracy and social immobility in its victims and has a pervasive role in Fridegård's work. Of his close to thirty novels and his nu-merous short stories and essays, most are autobiographical, de-picting the lives of lower-class working people.

Fridegård occupies an important place in modern Swedish lit-erature, and most critics consider his trilogy of novels about the young Lars Hård to be his best work. The first of the trilogy, *I, Lars Hård (Jag Lars Hård)*, caused a national furor when it ap-peared in 1935 because of its unusual candor and, to some, its un-relieved pessimism. But in the years following, its literary value could not be denied and it became recognized as a modern classic. Although the trilogy and many of Fridegård's other books have been translated into several European languages, this is the first English translation of any of his novels. Only three of his other works—short stories—are available in English: my translations of "100 Kilos Rye" (*Scandinavian Review*, June 1980), "Natural Selec-tion" (*Malahat Review*, July 1980), and "The Key" (*Translation*, April 1983).

*I, Lars Hård* put Jan Fridegård in the center of a social and political movement worldwide and a major literary movement in Sweden. Much influenced by such authors as Anton Chekhov, Maxim Gorky, Jack London, and Upton Sinclair [1] and coming from an oppressive milieu, Fridegård was well equipped to join his Swedish colleagues who wrote autobiographical novels revealing the horrible conditions under which many people lived. Eyvind Johnson and Harry Martinson, for example, who jointly won the Nobel Prize for literature in 1974, both wrote important proletarian works at the time, Johnson his tetralogy about Olof (1934–37) beginning with *1914* and Martinson his novel, *Flowering Nettle* (1935). Vilhelm Moberg, well known to English speakers for *The Emigrants*, also joined this movement with his Knut Toring trilogy (1935–39), translated as *The Earth Is Ours*. But it was Fridegård and two other writers of the period who formed a special subgroup of worker novelists, the statare school. Ivar Lo-Johansson, Moa Martinson, and Jan Fridegård helped expose their countrymen to the brutality and immorality of the statare system. They were doubtless partially responsible for Sweden's abolishing the system in 1945.

Important as that social change is, achieving it was not Fridegård's sole purpose. Although the statare system profoundly affected him and although he was strongly attracted to such patently didactic, and aesthetically weak, books as Upton Sinclair's *Samuel the Seeker*, his novel never descends to the level of political tract or propaganda. In fact, much of the richness we sense in *I, Lars Hård* derives from the balance between the implicit social criticism and the analysis of a human character in a social context. The book castigates society, to be sure, but its essential core, enmeshed in a weaving of pathos, irony, and ribald humor, sets it apart from many other class-conscious novels. Fridegård's steadfast refusal to give simple answers—despite the novel's apparent simplicity— helps make his work a classic.

That simplicity deserves some comment before we move on to the subtleties that distinguish the book, for it becomes part of a complex view on appearance and reality that Fridegård develops

1. Lars Furuland, "Fridegårds bildningsgång och bibliotek," *Svensk litteraturtidskrift* 33, no. 4 (1970): 25–39.

Introduction

throughout the work. The novel's form, for instance, immediately creates problems. Written in the first person, the narrative reaches us in a pure, evocative, sagalike form but without the saga's objectivity, without its claim to an omniscient and wise narrator. The novel's initial lightness, its vastly entertaining qualities, and its clear, easy pronouncements on good and bad make it compelling, persuasive reading, but Fridegård filters those observations through the detritus of Lars's own experience. As we come to know Lars, we come to distrust the initial impressions of the timeless battle between good and evil that he creates. A series of Chinese boxes enclosing one another, the novel never lets us settle too quickly on a single cause for Lars's dilemma.

Two controlling themes illustrate clearly how this complexity within simplicity is achieved and what it can accomplish: Lars's relationship to women and his relationship to nature. The first, of course, though sometimes amusing, is not always admirable and may account in part for the angry reception the novel first had, including a damning comparison by one critic to James Cain's *The Postman Always Rings Twice*, which appeared the year before.[1] Both books seem crude, nihilistic, morally dangerous. But Fridegård's novel strongly correlates the vagaries of sexual relations with the restrictions of society, endowing each with hypocrisy, deceit, and abuse as central characteristics. Lars's trysts with the three nameless upper-class girls obviously strengthen the correlation. He wishes to "bowl over—literally—with flattery" both the first and second girls, and so he comments sincerely on the profound or pensive looks in their eyes; he later denies to the brown-eyed, buxom girl that he ever had any real interest in the first one, obviously lying. Even in his unique and "faithful" relationship with the third girl, he lies about his relationships with the other two, and once, as she crawls in under the barn door, he feels compelled to kick her in the head, presumably out of class hatred. The sheer bulk of narrative devoted to these three girls thus argues for their importance to the novel's meaning. But significantly, a minor figure—from Lars's point of view, and that, of course, affects

1. Martin Rogberg, quoted in Erik Gamby, *Jan Fridegård: Introduktion till ett författarskap* (Stockholm: Svenska bokförlaget, 1956), p. 69.

ours—most profoundly influences his fate. The seemingly secondary Hilma Andersson becomes Lars's real nemesis. She takes on much more importance than he and we would have originally assumed, and for two specific reasons.

Hilma comes from the lower classes and she lives in the city. The first point is crucial because, despite her status, Hilma treats Lars as society does, and thus she becomes synonymous with the oppressive forces he associates with another class. Fridegård strengthens the parallel between society at large and Lars's peers by showing the same reaction to both: Lars hates the letters from Hilma and those from the child welfare bureau, the representative of society. A member of his own class defeats Lars in the class war symbolized by the battle between the sexes, a battle apparently mainly between him and the upper-class girls. This reveals the true enemy as not just the upper class, not just one faction of society dominating another, but the entire system. A product of society and therefore trapped by it, Lars is in some ways doomed to repeat the mistakes of his class and of the past, despite his efforts to extricate himself from both. Like his father, who fathered a child before he was married, Lars too is supposed to have fathered Hilma's child and thus doomed himself to a wretched life.

An equally important fact about Hilma forms the bridge to the novel's other controlling theme. Although she is from the lower classes, she is also from the city and so tied to the book's Rousseauian message. Whether Fridegård read Rousseau directly (e.g., *Contrat social, Lettre à d'Alembert sur les spectacles, Émile*) or became familiar with his ideas through the works of such authors as August Strindberg (i.e., in *The Red Room* or the short story "Remorse of Conscience") the essential Rousseauian dichotomy between the purity of nature and the degradation of society permeates *I, Lars Hård*. Fridegård clearly articulates it in the cave incident when "a man and a woman met the same way they had a thousand years ago, before nature's comedian and fool, the sparsely haired ape, invented society with titles, uniforms, and a thousand other outward manifestations of inward emptiness." By making Hilma the agent of Lars's fall and by associating her with the city, with destructive society and other "outward manifestations," Fridegård destroys the illusion that goodness or evil resides in one class alone. Lars's relationship to women, then, is never simple. While it seems a mere expression of animal lust at times, and at times it seems to cloak a deeper social message, even the second level of meaning only palely reflects the real social commentary. Fridegård further undermines the ostensible simplicity of the book and further highlights the perniciousness of society by his use of humor, miscellaneous detail, ironic allusion, and metafictional technique. The scene at the church dean's house, for instance, needs no explanation—"people are so nice at Christmas." And such details as Lars's recent dismissal from a city job for insubordination, his having spent three abominable years in the military, and the cleavage he feels between his "animal male" interior and his "cultural coat" all conform to the Rousseauian pattern. So does the offhanded allusion to Sven Duva. With that device, Fridegård at once calls into question Lars's insightfulness at the time he entered the military, since Sven is so stupid, and also mocks the unthinking patriotism that a book such as Runeberg's implies. Allusions to pulp literature or early films, as in the repetition of stylized, villainous laughter, "ha ha" and "ho ho,"[1] further intensify the criticism of a tradition run dry, not applicable to the contemporary Swedish, statare world. And such allusions naturally heighten the technical self-consciousness that characterizes much of the novel. Fridegård's references to "real novels" and "old and tried patterns" and his ironic reference to the nineteenth-century tradition of Dickens, Thackeray, and Dumas ("I won't ask the honorable reader . . .")[2] show that a new realism in literature should accompany the new awareness of the statare's plight. All these features form the intricate fabric of the novel's cultural and social criticism.

The multilayered, sometimes subtle, sometimes blatant attacks

---

1. Lars Forssell, "Jordiska prosa: En studie i Jan Fridegårds komposition," in *Jan Fridegård*, ed. Artur Lundkvist and Lars Forssell (Stockholm: Förlaget frilansen, 1949), p. 43.
2. Arne Häggqvist, "Fridegårds Lars Hård-stil," in Häggqvist, *Blandat sällskap* (Stockholm: Ars förlag, 1954), p. 134.

on society apparently stand in marked contrast to the relatively simple descriptions of nature. Nature is the book's still point, as Lars wishes it to be, and the style representing it differs considerably from that of the rest of the novel. The numerous references to nature are all characterized by a remarkable precision and accumulation of detail, from the mere naming of plants such as coltsfoot, anemone, tussilago, and bird cherries, to the description of colors, such as aniline-colored pine cones, and smells, such as the fern's musklike odor of sperm. These details give those portions of the book a concreteness and stability that the rest of the book, with its absence of names, definite places, and descriptions, lacks. Even the tone of the natural passages differs from the others, except when Lars imposes his own moods and perceptions on the scenes he describes, as when suffering hypocritically over the first girl's infidelity, he imagines every thicket calling "with its dark womb for some titillating sin." For although inevitably drawn to nature, Lars cannot fully understand or fully immerse himself in its saving powers because of his background and place in a social structure. While he associates even his own soul with natural metaphors, and while he seduces the three girls in natural settings apart from social strictures, his involvement in society, conscious and unconscious, prohibits him from separating himself from society as he would like. When he tries to become part of nature, "cowardly, sickly apprehensions cast their black shadows over everything" he feels. Nature—and personal fulfillment—are always just beyond his reach.

While this major theme is thus definitely more straightforward and direct than the sexual theme, the central character complicates our perception of nature, making that realm seem an impenetrable area for human beings. Lars, an inveterate outcast, socially unredeemed, is still a product of society, displaying much of the same degradation that divides it from nature. He is caught in a morass of self-contradiction and self-delusion. He denigrates society yet acts as manipulatingly and selfishly in his affairs with the three girls; he derides Hilma for wanting him to support her, but wants upper-class women to do the same for him; he mocks the deputy for his devotion to a cap, but covets the cap of university students;

Introduction

and he hates society for setting man against man, but divides the sexes just as arbitrarily and just as damagingly. Lars is hypocritical and pretentious, differentiating himself from his father while re-enacting parts of his father's life and even deriving much of his knowledge from the same source—Nordenmark. His bitterness, as well as his statare heritage, thus make him a familiar figure, akin to Jean in Strindberg's *Miss Julie*. Unlike Jean, however, Lars Hård also unwittingly shows an inner tenderness and capacity for human warmth belying his name, one more piece in the super-structure of appearance. In this novel his tenderness appears in lit-tle touches like his exchanging the small girl's spade for a lighter one when she is away and in his manifest love and compassion for the old man and woman. Though he displays public hardness later, pessimistically claiming he attended the old man's funeral only to get free coffee, his previous actions have shown his tre-mendous affection for both people. In the second novel of the tril-ogy, *Jacob's Ladder*, his capacity for tenderness becomes yet more pronounced. There he prays that God will be a little harsher with him just as long as He takes it a little easier on an old prisoner whom Lars has seen the same day. And in the last novel, *Charity*, Lars returns home to nurse his dying mother and find peace. Ap-pearance, in these novels as well as the first, is not always reality.

The opposition Fridegård sets up, then, between what is and what seems to be can cause difficulties in interpreting the novel. Indeed the book's pessimistic surface seduced early critics, and they condemned the book out of hand. Lars does in fact show lit-tle conscious development or improvement by the novel's last page, since there, as in the military, he vows to become as terrible as he is capable of being. But even if he and his critics have trouble seeing beneath his hard exterior, even if he cannot perceive his own connection to society and does not realize how his actions reflect those of the order he hates, nevertheless he does sense that something exists beyond the visible, possibly in nature, something that words cannot describe. These occasional visions of the ineffa-ble imply an ultimate hope; they also show that Lars's words, or-ganized by convention, cannot yet contain the vision that he and the dying, inarticulate old woman may have.

Like other classic Scandinavian novels with a social theme, such as Knut Hamsun's *Hunger*, Fridegård's book rises above the social and political message implicit within it and becomes a monument to art and to the human spirit. The surrogate "I" is oppressed, mostly by society but also by himself. By exploring the oppositions he creates in Lars Hård, Fridegård thus tells the story of hundreds in a political and social sense, but also, perhaps more significantly, in an emotional and a psychological one as well.

I, Lars Hård

Three girls walked past one of the statare[1] huts on the estate and looked in through the window. They were upper-class girls, dressed in men's clothes made of khaki. They had arrived a few weeks ago, and now people knew that they were going to learn about farming and gardening. The surplus of women nowadays makes it hard for everyone to marry well and so some have to strike out in new directions—at least that's what statare Hård's son Lars said, just returning from the city.

The girls looked through the window into the statare's cabin; they had probably heard that Lars was home and without work. What could he look like? He surely ought to have a little more go in him than the boys from the estate, who'd never been out in the world.

The first laughed, for no apparent reason, and said something to her friends right in front of the window. Lars noticed later that she always laughed when there were men around, even if they were middle-aged and married. She was tall and slender; her legs looked skinny inside her heavy socks. What you noticed most about her face was a pair of squinting, cheerful eyes and a row of glistening teeth. From behind, you could see she was a little bowlegged.

The second was more buxom and brown-eyed. She had thin lips and seldom smiled. She tried to peer into the statare's dark

1. See the Introduction.

3

kitchen, and from inside you saw her chest bulge under her blouse. Her buttocks were broad and her calves beautifully arched.

The third was small; she reached only to her friends' shoulders. Her appearance was undefinable, but you got an impression of blue when you looked at her. She smiled without looking in the window. Her forehead was broad and white, her nose turned slightly upward, and her glance was blue and firm. Like her taller friend, she too was a bit bowlegged.

I, Lars Hård, saw those three girls walk past our window. It was at the beginning of April, and I had just been fired from the factory for insubordination. All I owned was two nice suits, an overcoat, and a watch of yellow metal that looked like gold. When I saw those three girls outside the window, I was glad for those things and in some vague way associated them with the girls and with the approaching summer.

"It's not proper for well-bred girls to do men's work," said my mother, looking disapprovingly at the three of them. "They're probably just some sluts their parents didn't want to have at home."

Still, secretly, I thought that the first two could just as well be sluts but I hoped the little one was pure and without experience.

I, Lars Hård, who had dated at least twenty factory girls and had taken all of them from movie theater directly to bed, I couldn't get those three out of my head the whole afternoon. Three times I walked past the place where they worked, and I heard the slim one's laugh each time. The buxom one thrust her chest out and the little blue one looked past me, smiling towards the horizon. Her lower lip was a bit too large but you couldn't imagine her with a smaller one.

The third time I walked past them I realized I was making a fool of myself. I went in and stayed there until the tittering girls walked past my window in the April dusk. Then I went to the plot of land they dug in, tested their spades, and changed the little one's, which was heavy, for the brown-eyed's, which was lighter. And that was me, Lars Hård, and three upper-class girls.

A grass road with a set of tracks in it from the wagon wheels ran straight across the estate. Small coltsfoot suns already shone from the muddy ditch by the side of the road and the last of the melted snow slurped among last year's grass at the bottom of the ditch.

I walked that road at dusk every evening all the way to where the great, night-black forest with its mile-long saw of tree tops tore asunder the spring-bleached sky. Sometimes I heard the partridge's strident cry from out in the fields; it was the night's only sound except for the constant rippling of the ditch water. There began my relationship with the thin girl, and a banal beginning it was, too.

Already at a distance I could see a thin, gray figure in my path. She walked slowly and stared at the edge of the ditch. I was bareheaded and when I was right in front of her, I nodded.

"Good evening. Do you know where I might find some coltsfoot flowers growing?" she asked. "Someone said that this is where they grow."

"True. It's just that you can't see them at night. They close up when the sun goes down."

"Oh, how funny." And she laughed at the flowers' closing for the night. I, who had read many books on all kinds of subjects, was twenty-five years old, and had known many women, this is what I thought: You upper-class girls, and all women for that matter, you open for the night at the same time the flowers close. You spread your arms and legs out like white petals and wait with closed eyes for the night's silent pollinator. You are night blossoms.

I was pleased with the comparison I had made and decided to store it in memory.

Meanwhile, the girl had turned and begun to walk in the same direction as I was walking. A worker's daughter can't do that; she has to giggle and let herself be coaxed into following along if you don't know her, but a well-bred girl, because of her superiority, can be a little free without being misunderstood. When I got nearer to the well-bred girl later on I wondered what it was that made her better than the factory girls. The only difference I noticed was the quality of the underwear.

We quickly began beating around the bush. What should a well-bred girl and a lower-class, but normally gifted, man talk about if not about books and their authors? "Have you read this one or that one? You really should—it's very profound."

And the whole time we both knew very well that we were prey to each other. Hard up for well-bred boys, the girl had sought me out and she certainly wasn't about to surrender herself before singing the old song in concert with me. In the meantime, I started to talk about the greatness of the cosmos as I had read it in Nordenmark.[1] The girl looked at me out of the corner of her eye and her respect surely rose a bit. Finally, I offhandedly dropped in the Latin names for some plants that would sprout in April.

And I knew that all the prattle was leading up to something; it was the male's special way of impressing the female in the spring. Of course I had a soul, too, but it always fell silent in the presence of a woman. It let itself be heard only when the night stood quiet and no human being was within sight or hearing. At times like those, I always wanted something extraordinary—and that, I believed, was of the soul.

Besides, I felt a clear difference between soul and body, and Schopenhauer had no disciple in me. He needn't bother trying to convince me that such elevated, pure sensations as I felt had their roots and origin in that thick cranium covered with hair from the days of the apes, that carcass full of diverse, unpleasant apertures, or these long, sparsely haired legs, which carried the upper splendor over the spring-black fields. No, the soul was separate from all that and simply did it the honor of making its residence there for a time.

A few stars stuck holes in the clear gray sky. As I gazed at them, I told the girl about a star that was twenty thousand light years

1. Nils Nordenmark (1867–1962), a professor of astronomy and biographer of Swedish astronomers such as Celsius and Wargentin, wrote a history of astronomy in Sweden to 1800. He was one of the founding figures in the Swedish Society of Astronomy.

away. Could she comprehend that? The star, by the way, was called Mira.

As I said that, I turned fully towards her, knowing that I looked better from the front than in profile. My grandfather was Russian and had kindly bequeathed his grandson his thick Cossack nose.

"Mira," the girl responded, laughing again. "Just think, we had a cat named that at home. A black one with white paws."

A cat and a heavenly body a thousand times greater than the sun! I decided to talk about trivialities. "I saw you and your two friends the other day through the window and I noticed you especially."

"No, really?" the girl answered greatly interested, turning towards me. "Why is that?"

"I don't know. There's something about you that's captivating without a person's knowing exactly what it is."

The girl's eyes and teeth glistened and she began walking closer to me. A lead-gray cloud bank stood immobile far off in the north. It resembled a crocodile with open jaws. Imperceptibly, it changed into a giant lizard with a crested back from the Jurassic period. I didn't point the animal out for the girl but said instead, "Let me see your eyes."

"How come?" she asked again and stopped, turning towards me and smiling.

"You have peculiar eyes. You must have a lot of experience." And I shook my finger jokingly at her.

I looked through the April dusk into her eyes, which were beautiful as a sun-drenched, inch-deep rain puddle on a mountain is beautiful. No danger of drowning in them.

The girl squinted at me, happy she had such peculiar eyes and firmly resolved to enchant me completely with them. Her raincoat smelled of the upper class; otherwise I probably would have dared kiss her. Not that I wanted to, but she probably thought it was about time. Well, we hadn't parted company yet.

"Experienced!" she laughed. "It all depends on what you mean."

She thought I had meant something; she had no idea I just wanted to bowl her over—literally—with flattery.

For another half hour we tossed laughter and semi-erotic non-sense back and forth and suddenly we were standing in front of the estate's large, dark outbuildings. A heavy wind passed between them and we heard the cows' mooing and the rattling of their halters in the barn. A gray-white vapor hung over the manure pit and as we approached, a huge, ravenous dog emerged and rushed off into the darkness, rasping its claws against the ground. The girl gasped and gripped my arm with both hands. "Oh," she said.

There was nothing else to do but take hold of her. I drew her towards me and when I felt her breasts and legs, my respect vanished and there was only a woman left in my arms.

We kissed for a long time under a few dripping trees before she went in. "No, it isn't right," she mumbled occasionally. "What will you think of me?"

She said the same words that nineteen of the twenty factory girls had said. We agreed to meet the next night. After I kissed her, she didn't laugh any more but became dead serious.

Her father was a bank president; my father was a statare and had a black beard. My grandfather had fled from Russia and become a Swedish soldier. Who knows, maybe he was something important in Russia. The more I thought about that, the more likely it seemed to me that he was a count or a prince in his homeland. I was, in other words, no less a person than she was.

I stopped on the staircase, listening into the night. A little rivulet wept in the grass, and our big gray cat came silently out of the dark and rubbed itself against my leg. Then it sat down next to me and stared attentively at something I couldn't see out in the night.

Our kitchen still smelled of fried pork from the evening meal when I came in. The pork smell blended with the odor of sweaty feet rising from father's gaping boots by the fire. It wasn't disagreeable; it reminded me of childhood at home. Next to the boots was the cat dish with milk in it and a saucer with bits of food the cat had left. I slept on a wooden bench by the wall in the kitchen, and Father and Mother slept in the bedroom in their old

Gustavian louse palace,[1] bought at auction in 1897 for almost nothing.

I sat down at the dropleaf table without lighting the candle and tried to think about the girl I had just left. But I could only hold on to her for a second before she was driven away by a little figure who smiled towards the horizon when you met her. Her legs bent out a bit when you saw her from behind.

Some coltsfoot I had picked during the day stood in a glass on the table, smelling mildly of the spring ditch they had come from. Sometimes the corner cupboard or the dropleaf table gave out a loud cracking noise. Father had started snoring in the bedroom. When I looked in, Mother took hold of his shaggy, black head and turned it to the side so he'd be quiet. "There's milk in the bottle if you're thirsty," she said to me then in her gentle, sorrowful voice.

The old bench creaked worse than hell when I lay down. A rat was nibbling away behind the wood bin and I thought apathetically that I could have taken the cat in with me.

Father started snoring again and I couldn't fall asleep. The kitchen reminded me of so much that evening that my thoughts soon wandered back to my childhood.

Yes, those were the days when a kid came bawling into the world in our family every other year. The kid would suck at Mother's breast for six months, drink milk for three, eat gruel for another three, and then be ready to dig into herring and potatoes.

My earliest memory was of a chimney sweep holding me on his knee and chewing for me from a saucer. In statare homes everywhere, you chewed for the kids before their own teeth came in. The chimney sweep's name was Sundvall; he was a childhood friend of my father's. When I got bigger, I couldn't stand him because he had chewed for me. When he was drunk, he always reminded me about it and laughed with huge, now toothless jaws.

---

1. A bed in the Gustavian mode, named after Sweden's King Gustav III (1746–92). Such beds were inexpensive and therefore rather common in statare dwellings.

The flue brush and soot ball lay on the staircase and more than once I made up my mind to hit him in the head with his own soot ball. But I never actually did it.

My father owned an old edition of *The Wonder of the Universe*,[1] which he read from often, and with one quotation from it he would silence all differences of opinion. He constantly stressed the insignificance of man in comparison with the universe and enjoyed thinking about how his master meant no more than he did from geological, biological, and many other standpoints. "He won't make a bigger clod of dirt than I will," he said. "What is man? No more than fly shit!" And he looked triumphantly at his children and wife.

Between the ages of twelve and seventeen, I went to the barn every day to curry the cows. With an iron currycomb I scratched the night's memories from their thighs and hocks until the sunshine, streaming through the dirty windows, looked like firm, slanted pillars of dust. I grew several inches each year, and in the last one, without a ladder I could observe interesting things about the life of spiders on the barn's roof.

Oh, yes, and then came the dreams about the future. I decided to become something. When the autumn peered grayly through the darkness of the barn's windows for the fifth time, I went to my father and announced my decision.

"What are you going to be?" my father asked, looking me up and down.

I don't know if my beak was as broad as Sven Duva's,[2] but history repeated itself in my answer. "Well, a soldier."

My father tried to convince me that I ought to stay home and do my military service like normal people and not run off and enlist.[3] But I wouldn't give in. Luckily, in the middle of the discus-

1. Nordenmark's popular account of astronomy published in 1910.

2. Sven Duva is a huge, dim-witted peasant boy in the collection of patriotic poems entitled *The Tales of Ensign Stål* by Johan Ludvig Runeberg (1804–77). Incapable of anything else, Sven becomes a soldier, bumbling but loyal, and manages to die heroically.

3. Sweden has had a draft system, in some form or other, for centuries. At this time (1919–25), all able-bodied men between the ages of eighteen and forty-seven had to serve in the military. They could fulfill their obligation by serving a total of 165 days in the infantry.

sion my father recalled *The Wonder of the Universe*. "Oh, well," he said with a sigh, "do what you want. Everything's moving towards some unknown goal and all you can do is follow along. What is man? Barely fly shit."

And he took out a pinch of snuff and walked away from me, satisfied with his words.

Then came the three years I spent in the cavalry, disgraceful years of unending rivalry to be the crudest among the crude. Filth, brawls, and favoritism worse than anywhere else. Bullying, masturbation, and syphilis.

Earlier I had often dreamed about the moment when I would hold a girl in my arms for the first time. She would be good, shy, and noble, and only reluctantly would she surrender to me. Oh, how it turned out instead.

When I came to the regiment, I had never so much as touched a woman. I had just stopped suspecting the midwife of carrying the baby with her in her black bag. Since then I've noticed that those particular feelings awaken much later in large boys than in those who are small. We live for the time being in an era of dwarfed aggressors. The big, powerful, but slow man can't keep up with the rest; by the time he steps forward, the table is cleared and the women impregnated, and so he's doomed to extinction. Or so I thought and that gave me at least some consolation.

I'd been in no more than two weeks when there was a dance one Saturday night in the gymnasium. There were just about as many girls as guardsmen, girls ugly and beautiful, with short hair and long skirts and vice versa. I stood in a corner and longed for home. Then suddenly the fiddler yelled, "Ladies!"

A rather tall girl in a red dress steered towards me where I stood with my back against the wall.

"May I?" she asked.

"I don't know how to dance."

"You don't? Well, then I won't dance the ladies' dance either. Besides, it's so warm inside. Shall we go for a walk instead?"

We went for a walk instead. The November evening was dark and misty. We walked down towards Djurgårdsbrunn cove,[1] and I

1. An area northeast of Stockholm.

searched the whole way for something to talk about. The girl was silent too.

We stopped by the bridge and listened to the wolves and owls hooting in Skansen.[1] A lighted barge went by. And then another.

The girl suddenly threw her arms around me without the least word of warning. She hid her face near the third button of my shirt and stood quietly, breathing a little laboredly. I stood and held out my arms while I sought frantically for something to say. The woman's touch woke no sensations in either my jacket or my pants. "Do you have a telephone?" I finally asked.

The girl made a movement with her head that could very well have been a nod.

"Then I can call you," I continued, holding out my arms.

In the same instant we heard voices right next to us and the girl let go of me. We both looked toward the voices. A gas lantern by the bridge hissed slowly, and in its glow we saw a corporal with his girl walking by on the shore. They stopped by a small tree a few steps away without seeing us. The corporal was pressing on, the girl resisting. "No, it's too crazy. Come home with me instead," she said. "It's just too wet on the ground."

"I don't have leave," answered the warrior without retreating. He threw his arms around both the girl and the tree, and her protestations died away. The young tree rustled slowly and rained its last leaves down accusingly over the latter-day Adam and Eve.

Here I had my shy, noble women. I didn't know then that one of the big city's sewage pipes went directly to the barracks.

The girl in the red dress walked away from me back towards the dance hall. I knew she was looking for someone who knew women better than I did.

I waded through those three years in any event, and then came the factory with its cleaner air, despite the nine hundred workers, half of either sex.

And now this girl tonight, the upper-class girl; from all appearances, I should get a little affair out of her. I wonder if I could

1. An outdoor museum in Stockholm with a small zoo and examples of architecture from various periods of Swedish history.

get someone like her to marry and support me. But what if I got her into trouble? Oh well, then her father would send her to Germany and send me a nasty letter.

Why can't I sleep tonight? I damn both poor and rich, what was and what will be. But if that small blue-eyed girl were walking along the road one evening. . . .

From coltsfoot to wild anemones is just a few days. But wild anemones don't grow on ditch banks; they grow under spruce trees. Both flowers close towards evening, though, and in rainy weather. I had a flashlight; under its light we picked the wild anemones, the thin girl and I. She loved them very much and showed it by uttering many little cries over them, but instead of taking them home, she forgot them on a rock.

The forest grew on a slope down to the lake. The water was still covered with blue-gray ice except along the shore, where a clear, black band of water glistened. It was absolutely quiet in the forest, but the silence was strangely full of life and procreation. We saw a black bird sitting on the ground, and after standing motionless for a long time watching, we saw it move a little. Finally we sneaked up closer to it. It didn't fly away. The girl clapped her hands and still it didn't fly away. It was a rotten boot.

The girl's laugh, ringing loudly through the waterside forest, was answered by the first ducks, quacking far away by the shore where the reeds would soon be shooting up.

"I know a cave in the forest a little ways from here," I said to the girl.

"Let's go and look at it," she answered spiritedly, laughing.

"Yes, come on."

I took her hand and we half walked, half ran through the dusk. The cave lay pretty deep in the forest, five or six feet back under an overhanging boulder. The ground was dry inside and I dragged the girl in with me.

We sat panting on the ground beside each other. The night was gray and warm outside the cave opening. The crescent of the moon lay somewhere behind the clouds.

I had had a very simple plan in mind when I suggested going to the cave. The ground was dry inside. But the strong, solitary, primordial atmosphere there made me forget about that.

There was something mystical about the cave. The first time I went to the forest it was in, I was seven years old, but I went straight to the cave as if I had known all about it. Even now it struck me that I had been here sometime before, thousands of years ago. I always turned instinctively when I went in, but the girl scraped her back on the rock and fell flat on the ground. I had to pluck the pine needles from the insides of her hands while she whimpered like a kitten.

The girl wanted to smoke but I didn't like that—cave women didn't smoke. But it gave me an idea. "Let's build a fire in the cave and pretend it's two thousand years ago," I suggested.

"Yes, let's," said the girl.

"You are another wild man's woman, home alone. My jacket can be the bearskin on your bed. Your wild man is out hunting. Then I come and want to steal you away but you protect yourself like the devil. All right?"

"Yes, yes," the girl answered with gleaming eyes, laughing.

I gathered a pile of sticks and twigs together and managed to get it lit with a pair of dunning notices I had in my pocket. The smoke curled soft and gray among the rocks. I saw threats of legal measures char together with company envelopes. The primeval days had returned now: a cave, a fire, a woman, and a man. No dunning notices.

"You sit and stare into the fire and wait for your shaggy wolf of a man," I said to the girl, creeping out.

I took my hat off outside, ruffled up my hair, and put a hanging lichen in my mouth so it looked like a full beard. Thus equipped, I sneaked back toward the cave, lay down, stuck my head in, and let go an extraordinary roar. The beard fell to the ground.

Before I had time to get up, the woman was on top of me. She threw her whole weight across my neck and mercilessly pressed my face against a pine cone on the ground. It hurt and I gave a sudden jerk so powerful that the prehistoric woman let go her hold and went rolling down on the bear skin.

Now I had to drag her out of the cave. I was completely taken up in my role and really intended to drag her out. But she fought furiously, silent but wild-eyed. I couldn't get her out of the place.

During the fight I felt a completely new sensation. The fire was dying down, but it still glowed faintly on the girl's legs, which were visible above the knees. The battle took another turn and I didn't think any more about letting go of my prey. If you steal something and take it away with you, that's theft, but if you take something and eat it up on the spot, that's pilfering. I decided on the latter.

To the very end, the cave woman fought the invader; she tore out more than half his hair and scratched a bloody stripe across his cheek. Even when she couldn't go on any longer, when her chest heaved up and down, she still had that happy rage in her eye. And when by brute force I parted her legs, she closed her eyes, probably to keep from seeing the odious intruder, and when she opened them again, she was only a somewhat shamefaced modern girl, pulling down her skirt and looking at herself in the flap of her purse. I was taken aback and a bit remorseful. "Why didn't you say that . . . that you were still a virgin?" I asked.

"That wouldn't have helped much," the girl answered.

But I wasn't too happy. I blew on the fire and put the beard, together with some sticks and spruce cones, on it. Then I sat down to brood and stare into the fire. Damn it! I was old-fashioned in my views, and I thought that when a woman had only one specimen of the red flower, she shouldn't let it go to just any amateur investigator who happened to pass by. Of course, there was an extenuating circumstance in this case: I was the botanist.

"Look," the girl said in a voice between laughing and crying, "it's your own fault; but the bearskin—it's really messed up now . . . ."

Outside, a spring wind swept through the forest and the slender spruce trees swayed and whispered. Here and there a great rock lay motionless like a giant, resting, prehistoric animal. The stumps stood empty as wastepaper baskets and the snakes would surely waken soon from their winter sleep under the dead roots. The girl's chin and cheeks shone white beneath her hat and she didn't say a word all the way home.

Our hut lay black and humble among the trees a short distance from the sprawling manor house, its row of windows glaring out into the night. The girl snuggled up against me and asked, "You don't think it can be dangerous do you—the consequences?"

The tip of her nose was cold, my feet were frozen, and I wanted to go home. "No, no, it's usually not risky the first time. But if your monthlies don't come on time, all you do is heat up some beer to drink. That usually hurries them along."

That was the simplest remedy I had heard the factory girls describe.

"How come you know about these things?" the upper-class girl asked, staring at me.

"Yes, well—uh—damn it—there was this guy who talked about it once."

"I see, a guy, sure. But now be nice and brush off my back."

I brushed her off with my hand, picked the pine needles out of her hair, and watched her sneak in through the door. Her father was a bank president; my father was a statare, but in the cave, a man and a woman had met the same way they had a thousand years ago, before nature's comedian and fool, the sparsely haired ape, invented society with titles, uniforms, and a thousand other outward manifestations of inward emptiness. Or so I, who was twenty-five years old, thought on a night that added yet another experience to those I had before.

In addition to the important task of driving the master and his family around, an estate's coachman also has the job of delivering up all the news about people on the farm to the master. The statare's stern god had deemed that we should be front-porch neighbors with the coachman. He was a man over fifty years old with a drooping yellow moustache, watery, slush-blue eyes, and an unquenchable interest in everything that happened on the farm. He would turn a bad piece of gossip into a scandal, filling in all gaps in the story from his own resources. He consequently grew old in general esteem and was awarded a medal for faithful service.

The front-porch door squeaked and creaked when you walked through it, and the coachman soon learned that I was out half the nights. His next task, which he immediately undertook, was to learn who I was out with. One night when the girl and I walked by our cabin towards the manor house, I saw his moustache flutter in the window among the flower pots, and I knew my goose was cooked. I prepared the girl for the landowner's inevitable wrath. At their parents' request, he also served as moral overseer for the three girls. Many years of frequent nighttime study tours to the maids' quarters had made him particularly well suited to the task.

The coachman was a widower and had a housekeeper. She was in her fifties too and weighed five times her number of years. She stood by him faithfully day and night and watched with him now to see who I came home with, a working girl or a girl from the upper classes. What's more, she kept her ear to our door in case some drama, worthy of being handed down to posterity, might play itself out at our place. Cleanliness was a concept unknown to her; she washed her coffee cups, her nose, and her mouth with the same dishrag. She saw no need to wash her hands because she baked once a week.

Otherwise she was hospitable and goodhearted. Her house was a tramps' Eldorado and they recommended her warmly to their colleagues who trod the surrounding roads. Sometimes her good heart would embrace me too.

One day as I was walking across the front porch, a sizzling noise and an odor emerged from the coachman's kitchen, and the housekeeper's voice called out to me. "Lars, come on in!"

I went in. The woman had planted her huge bulk before the

stove, and with a knife she was turning some things in the frying pan.

"You'll have a potato pancake, won't you?" she offered. "They're really good, you bet. Here, sit down on the sofa and have one."

All my objections about having just eaten meant nothing to that greasy palace of pork, and she came swaying towards the sofa with a potato pancake on the knife, supporting it with the black fingers of her left hand.

She laid the bit of food in my outstretched hands and topped it with a clump of lard that started to melt immediately from the warmth, creating a lake on top of the potato pancake.

There I sat, the old woman looking benevolently at me through the smoke and waiting for me to sing the pancake's praises.

I nibbled on an edge of it and smacked my lips so that she would think it was good. A moment passed and when the old woman turned back towards the stove, I quickly dropped the potato pancake behind the sofa and sighed with satisfaction.

But I sighed too soon. The cat, sitting on the floor, pricked up its ears when the pancake plopped down. Then it got up and moved with interest under the sofa. I tried to stop it with my foot but failed.

There was a shuffling sound, and the cat's tail emerged. The animal came out backwards, dragging the potato pancake, full of spider webs, with it. When the pancake was out, the cat dropped it and looked first at the old woman and then at me, licking its chops.

"Time to go," I said and got up. "I'm in a bit of a hurry."

"Yes, get out of here and be quick about it if you think you're too good to eat that up," said the housekeeper, assuming a threatening stance. "And don't expect any favors from me just because you're messing around with the rich girls at night . . . ."

I managed to get back to our hut. From the coachman's kitchen I heard the housekeeper praise the cat for its good conduct. The next day neither she nor the coachman responded to my greeting.

I went to my father and complained about evil, stupid, and simple people. What had I done to hurt them?

"The hell with them," counseled my father. "In fifty years all three of you will be six feet under. What good will their jaw flapping do then? What is man? No more than a piece of fly shit. Never mind about them."

Wood anemones had taken over the pasture land, and the fields were full of dust from the iron limbs of the machines they were using to open the earth's womb and sow the seeds that clattered down from the wandering red box.

The road went over a little ridge in the newly harrowed field, and there I saw some round, green objects in the earth. They were silver and copper coins dating back to the sixteenth century and up to the nineteenth. I picked them up and went to an old man who was born on the farm and had never been away for more than the two weeks he drilled as a recruit at Polacksbacken in Uppsala. "Do you know if there were ever any houses up there on the hill?" I asked him. "If people ever lived there?"

"People? Yes, you better believe it. The distillery used to be there, you know. Torn down when I was a serving boy. In '55, if I recollect."

"I've just found some old coins over there in the field."

"Yeah, lots of people do. I've got some coppers here I found just after they tore the distillery down some seventy years ago. Want to see them?"

The old man breathed heavily as he took out an old case with bone work around the keyhole and showed me a handful of coins.

"Are you going to sell them?"

"No, I'll hold on to them. Whenever I see them I think of how we used to drive home from the field with the oxen. Sometimes when we were right in front of the distillery, Brännarlasse would come out with a ladle of brandy for us. He was a good man, that distiller. Now instead of the distillery, all we have is gray fields. For a long time I knew which grave was Brännarlasse's, but now it's been more than fifty years since he died, so he had to give his grave up for someone else a year or two ago." [1]

The old man was silent for a moment and then went on.

"I couldn't keep from going to the churchyard and seeing when they'd put a new body in Brännarlasse's place. There weren't many bones left. It goes faster when there's gravel mixed in with the dirt like there is here. It was strange anyway. I did see an armbone though, and I got to thinking that it might have been that very one that offered me a ladle of brandy some years ago."

"Do you think that piece of bone was all there was left of him?"

"Yes—well, I mean, apart from some tiny splinters and a little piece of skull that looked like a dirty plate."

"Yes, but don't you think he's alive anyway?"

"Are you crazy, boy? You think Brännarlasse's alive?"

"Not his body, of course, but the invisible part, the soul?"

"If it can't be seen, it can't live either," the old man answered confidently. "Why should it go on living when it's dead? I don't want any part of that salvation they talk about in the Bible, not me. If I'm going to live any longer, I want to be here where I know my way around. But then I'll want to be young again and work, drink, fight, and sleep with women. What good is it otherwise?"

But I was young and life was powerful within me; I wanted to live no matter what. I couldn't reconcile myself with the fact that my noteworthy self would disappear, that a time would come when I wouldn't exist any more. I said a dejected good-by to the old man, who nodded to me with a pinch of snuff in one hand and the birch-bark box in the other.

Walking across the fields, I was startled by the sunshine—silent, eternal, and rich—that spread out over the vast expanses as far as I could see. Far off in the distance towards the forest, the sower's red box continually wandered back and forth in the shimmering

---

1. According to a 1916 law, a Swedish citizen could have a burial plot in a churchyard or public graveyard only by written permission. The owner retained rights to the plot either in perpetuity or for a designated period of not more than fifty years. The church or community authorities could then assign the plot to someone else.

heat. A large, somnolent fly came and sat on my sun-drenched chest. I slowed down and let it stay there until it flew away of its own free will. I didn't want anything to die; if I were God, I would give life and enlightenment to match the desire of everything—flies, frogs, pigs, and people.

It was nearly the end of April and the joy of the earth was intense. I walked past some spruce trees, which sought in vain to hold on to their sullen dignity. The resin poured forth its fragrance and aniline-colored cones in the treetops told tales of inner gladness. I tried to force my way in and become part of it, but cowardly, sickly apprehensions cast their black shadows over everything I felt.

I met a boy on his way to the store. I tried to get him to share my pessimism, but he grinned and said, "That's how bleak and gloomy everything gets when you sleep with women too often. I know the signs. You shouldn't do it more than once a week at the most. They think that's too little, of course, but I don't give a damn about that."

He talked nonsense, that country bumpkin. Had he ever had a factory job or so much as touched a well-bred girl? Had he ever read a word of philosophy? No, he totally lacked the qualifications for understanding a soul like mine.

He could grin as much as he wanted. Here he was anyway, doomed to walk around in this godforsaken place until he got some girl in trouble. Then he would have to get married and become a statare while I on the other hand . . . I on the other hand . . . .

What the hell did I have on the other hand? Wasn't it just as good to have a well-ordered internal life like that guy there as to carry around the chaotic refuse heap that I carried, pride floating above it like green slime on the stinking water of a stagnant swamp?

I left the boy and continued to upbraid my soul, my body, and all my perceptions until I got home. I wondered if there was another person in the world who was as big, unhappy, and misunderstood as I was. I looked at my mother with a look burdened by fate and wondered if she would ever be able to understand who she had given birth to. "Mama, did anything special happen around the time I was born?"

Mother thought.

"Special? Well, yes. The cat ran away," she recalled. "The fox probably got in and took it. And Mrs. Svenson, the lady next door, twisted her ankle, but she was always running around like an idiot . . . ."

"No, I mean was there anything in the newspapers about some comet or shooting star or something?"

Mother thought again.

"Oh, I remember a shooting star but that was when I was just a girl. Stars fell like rain but none came down in this area here. But such things must be in your books somewhere. What can I say? I couldn't stand that Svenson lady but I had to help her anyway because when I came up, there she was lying there; and you, you bawled night and day. I've never heard the like for bawling in a kid. But I've never seen any comet."

That was all I got to know about the signs and marvels of the year of my birth. I bawled worse than other kids.

That night I had to walk alone under the moon. I knew the rumor had reached its destination and the protector of innocence had intervened. "Ha, ha, too late," I said inwardly, thinking about what had happened in the cave. I went back there and crept in, lit a match, and looked at the traces of the battle. If I could get the smallest one here, I thought, I'd make the bed with spruce twigs for her—no—with ferns. Ferns smell so provocative; they have the musk-like odor of sperm. Maybe protoplasm smelled that way or at least the primal cryptogam forests.

It was there she had lain on my coat, the slender rich girl. Would she remember that when she got married to some bigwig? Think how innocent she'll look when he tries to pump her about her experiences. And she'll be right in keeping quiet; women seem to have some idea how hellishly a man can suffer from their talk of earlier tumbles. Does the woman suffer worse? Oh no—with her, safety valves open all over her body, but a man, he swallows and swallows without outlet . . . .

So I thought in the cave. It was absolutely calm and the spruce trees stood immobile outside. In the end, I detached myself completely from everything outside. I vaguely remembered towns, houses, and something called people. It was so quiet it roared. I sat for a long time and listened. Water was dripping somewhere, regularly. Drip . . . drip . . . drip. Suddenly a feeling of terror formed deep in my being and I moved dizzily through millions of years of silence or millions of miles of emptiness, I don't know which, but I turned ice-cold and my head tingled and my hair stood on end. I rolled out of the cave, came up on my legs, and gasped . . . God . . . God . . . . I ran through the forest, every breath a whistling groan. Eternity had opened momentarily before a mosquito, and it tried whimperingly to save what it had up until then called its reason.

At the edge of the forest I stopped and tried to swallow my heart. The village slept before me and I began to reestablish contact with my former self. Somewhere behind my being the terror refused to die, even though I could sneer at myself when I thought of hopping and running through the forest, a little something fleeing in terror from a big nothing.

I walked across the field and thought that death would be a warm and peaceful deliverance if that vague terror ever returned, intent on staying. To get back to normal, I tried calling the girl to mind, but she danced away like a little speck of dust in the empty universe. The camphor drops, I thought then. Mother has camphor drops. And I felt relieved to think about the little bottle with the camphor smell.

Still full of anguish, I saw the coachman's moustache flutter in the window, and through the wall I heard him talk with his woman in an injured tone. He was complaining about my impudence: I had kept him awake half the night and then had come home alone. An interesting detail, of course, was that I had come as if the devil were on my heels.

With quivering hands, I looked in the sideboard among the castor oil, cordial, stomach medicine, and antacid drops until I got hold of the camphor drops.

"Are you sick?" Mother's gentle voice asked from the bedroom. "Toothache."

"If it's a cavity, you should stick in a cotton swab with some drops on it. It's hard to have a toothache at night. Try to get some sleep anyway."

"All right."

The cat lay on my bed, and it started kneading and purring ingratiatingly when I lay down. He probably sensed I wouldn't have the nerve to throw him out.

"Wrap a wool scarf around your head," Mother's voice called out again from the bedroom.

Chewing on a piece of sugar soaked in camphor, I thought about how gentle a woman's voice sounds in the night. A mother's voice anxiously gentle, a lover's voice caressingly gentle. And I thought that it was probably good for us men to have them. I decided to appreciate them more than I had up until then. Yes, for the moment I was even tempted to think of them as equal to myself. But I quickly saw the untenability of such a position.

Mother raised her voice from the bedroom yet one more time. "There's a letter on the table," she said. Father snored heftily.

A letter was very unusual and I got up and lit our size-fourteen kerosene lamp so I could read it. It was badly written on the outside, crooked and slanting, one consonant hitting the other in the jaw. I turned it over several times with a vague feeling of uneasiness. Finally I got up my courage and opened it.

Deer Mr. Lars Hård,

Now its true that wen we were together last autum my monthlees didnt come afterwords. So thats how it is. Oh youll probably deny it of course but that wont work. Now days men get nailed no matter how much they fight. So dont deny it. Now we can eether move in together or you can coff up sum mony. Im no uglier than other girls.

As ever,
Hilma Andersson

I froze, but I was standing with just a shirt on too, so that could be why. The cat squinted cordially at me and some flies began buzzing with joy above the lamplight. I read the letter again, put out the light, and lay down. The fear that came over Nain[1] was a cry of joy compared to what I felt.

Over and over again until the gray light of morning came in, my fearful and tired brain reconstructed the events of the fall. Could it be me? No—I had gotten a little drunk and nothing had happened. We hadn't even been alone together. We had met when I was home visiting one time.

I'd heard five others talk about having her, three guys and two married men. Hilma Andersson was home to visit, too, and she, of course, wanted to show the farmers that a Stockholm girl wasn't like the sweethearts out in the country. Wonder if each of those five got a letter like mine all his own.

Towards morning, I decided to write and appeal to the woman's possibly noble feelings and to freshen her memory about those five other men. I composed the letter in my head—a cold politeness should make her impudence sink down into her boot tops. Then she'd probably turn to someone who stood—or lay—closer to her than I did.

I remember clearly she had spent a whole night with one of those married men when his wife was away. A lot of people had seen her go home in the morning. Why didn't she blame him? He had a good position and no children. And those three guys had been with her many times, but she didn't accuse them. Only poor me, who'd only messed around with her a little when I was half drunk. I clearly remember she had horrible breath; I wasn't too drunk for that. But a girl who's had different men every night probably can't remember who really has been close to her.

Oh, well, she can try to summons me; I'll tell the court everything and be acquitted. Move in together, she thinks. If she moved in with everyone she's slept with, she'd have to rent a tenement house. The devil should move in with her—I wasn't about to.

Just think if it got around the village. That would be just fine.

---

1. See Luke 7:11–16. Jesus raises a man from the dead in Nain, bringing fear on the entire city.

As if there weren't enough talk about me already. I had rotten luck, that's all. I didn't get a wink of sleep that night either.

I've tried to live like a human being according to a philosophical formula for many years now, but people wouldn't leave me alone. Damn it! I can't keep my hands off women who offer themselves up right in front of me. What's so strange about that? It's probably the same with all men but they're just more cunning than I am. I walk a straight road and don't sneak. Yes, that's the way I am.

I ruminated further and found that people were more false, more horrible, and more heartless than I'd ever considered them before. Gentlemen and workers—the same bastards. I didn't fit in anywhere, with the high or with the low. It was the same with Nietzsche and Beethoven.

On and on my thoughts danced in the dark of the kitchen.

The greatest souls don't have the usual social graces. They have too much inside. So they're the laughingstock of the masses, the common men. Yes, I myself was a living example. When I was home at Christmas the year before, I was going to the church dean's on an errand. They were just going to have some coffee, and they invited me to join them even though my father was a statare. People are so nice at Christmas. It was the dean with his family and a couple of lady guests.

In fact, it was all a bunch of crap. In front of every coffee cup lay a huge buck made of gingerbread with sugar icing. And Christmas tree candles too. I'd never seen anything like it before. First I dunked a couple slices of saffron bread, poor devil that I am, and then I ate up the buck, flesh and hide, bones and innards. I dunked a leg, then the horn, and then the tail in the coffee and didn't stop so long as the least bit of buck was left on earth.

When I was done, I looked around. All of them had stopped drinking coffee and were sitting with strangely tense faces. Everyone still had his buck left, but where mine had been was an awful, empty space. No doubt any longer; I had consumed the table decoration. It hadn't occurred to me for a moment that the bucks could have served any other purpose than to be eaten up.

The dean's son told a poor joke, and everyone laughed wildly at it. "It's sure a good thing you got to laugh," I thought bitterly. "Otherwise you all would've burst, and I would have had to swim for my life."

What more is there to say? The dean's maid told the story in the parish and it got me a lot of disgrace. I explained everything to my father and complained about my constant bad luck.

"A buck," answered my father, "is basically the same as a ram. The constellation of the Ram covers an immense expanse. What's a damned gingerbread buck compared to that? What's the dean himself compared to that, for that matter? Hardly fly shit. Never mind about them."

The upper-class girl didn't come back even though the evenings were light and warm and there was tender green grass to lie in. Alone, tall, and bitter, I stalked through the fields and disappeared into the forest every night. I carefully avoided the cave with its eternal dripping.

My friendship with the second girl, the one with the brown eyes and full bust, began as a consequence of the first. She came up the road one evening with greetings from her friend, who said I should come to her window at eleven o'clock. She wasn't al-lowed out at night without an escort ever since we had been seen coming out of the forest together after midnight. Now she had something to tell me at the window.

That's what the girl said, very understanding about the situa-tion. She belittled the landowner and his wife for not letting them do as they pleased and thinking they couldn't take care of them-selves. She would have walked out right under their noses if it had been her. That's how she was and always had been.

After the girl had said all this, looking at me with her brown eyes, she stood pondering. She was dark skinned and had raven-black bangs on her forehead. She was buxom and smelled of the upper class and women. I had heard that her father was a high-ranking official in the service of the state. Now I wondered silently where she stood intellectually, whether I should talk about Emer-son, spring, or herself. I decided in favor of the latter as the only subject where you can never go wrong.

At the edge of the forest lay a little croft, red and friendly; we heard voices and the clatter of milk buckets from it. A cat glided like a white dot between the cottage and outbuilding. I looked at the girl and said, "Forgive me for saying this to you, but you have such profound, pensive eyes. For your age. I noticed them the first time I saw you."

"When was that?"

"The first day I was home, I saw three ladies walking past our window—that is, I saw only one—you."

The girl stood silently, looking towards the sunset, which colored her completely brick-red. But she didn't say a thing and she didn't go home. Such a strange one.

"You look like a painting by Millet when you stand like that looking out over the fields," I said. "If only the grain were yellow all around you."

I had thought carefully first and had pronounced the French painter's name correctly.

"Why are you saying these things to me?" the girl asked quietly. "It's my friend, after all, that you're—you're interested in."

"Yes, well, I guess that means we've walked here on the road and talked a few evenings. Interested? Well, I don't know . . . ."

"Oh no, don't deny it. The interest's obviously mutual, for that matter."

"If I only dared to say . . . ."

"Say what?"

She was finally a little gentler. She had turned towards me and her eyes were warmer. Her blouse stretched over her chest and her hands were too broad for an upper-class girl.

"Well?" she asked, having completely forgotten about her friend.

"Yes, well, that it was you the whole time I wanted to get to know. But you never came. So your friend turned into a kind of greeting, a breath of air from you, you see. Shall we walk a little?"

The girl didn't answer but when I started walking, she did too. She looked at the ground, but it was obvious anyway that she thought herself too good to walk with me, that it was only an experimental diversion for her. Maybe she'd tell her friend everything I'd said when she got home.

28

I thought of telling about the star Mira but, after further consideration, decided not to. In any case, I said something about the ice age when we passed a jagged boulder, but she didn't show any livelier interest. Then I took the last way out; I asked her why she hadn't gotten into the movies. As far as I could see, she would have been successful there.

Then the girl finally raised her eyes from the tips of her toes to my face. Oh, yes, she wouldn't deny that she'd been nursing such plans and had even sent in her picture. It was, for that matter, extraordinary, but everyone thought as I did. Oh, yes, she'd thought of becoming a star, of course, but her parents were against it.

"A star of the first magnitude," I thought and looked at her substantial accessories, which bounced both in the front and in the back.

We found sponge mushrooms, looked at an anthill, and climbed up on a mountain. On the ledges of the mountain, she took my hand for help; her skirt was pulled up tight over her knees when she climbed. I thought of telling her she looked like a painting from *La Vie Parisienne* but didn't when I wasn't sure of the pronunciation; she may have known French. In the meantime, the image of the slender girl completely faded away before this one's more palpable exterior.

There was no ravenous dog friendly enough to scare her into my arms, but it was my view, grounded in experience, that you shouldn't let a woman go away unkissed if you didn't want to earn her contempt. I had every reason to move a little quickly. I remembered all too well one night when I had sat properly on a blanket next to a girl in Kaknäs forest;[1] I had sat the whole night without touching her. When it was dark in the forest, she looked good, but when the gray morning light filtered down, she was blue-red in the cheeks and not the least bit enticing.

She said a respectful good-by and walked bouncing her bottom over Ladugård field towards town. I rolled up my blanket and went home feeling there would never be any real guardsman in me. I didn't have the knack.

1. Northeast of Stockholm, across the canal from Djurgården.

A week or two later, she got her revenge. After having gathered together six like-minded girls among the hundred who joggled and danced to the jazz music in the gymnasium, she came up and stood in front of me, curtsied, and amid her friends' derisive laughter asked, "I'd like to know when you're coming home to take my virginity from me."

The nearest guardsmen heard everything, and the "ha ha's" and "ho ho's" mixed in with the girls' "hi hi"-ing. I searched for an abusive word for a moment but couldn't find one that seemed strong enough. Among gaping jaws that shot out sounds defying all musical scales and laws, I walked out into the open air.

That was what I got for my chivalrous inaction on the blanket. I learned from the incident and bettered myself.

I thought about that story, noting within how hard it is to know where you have a woman. The one walking here looking reserved, for instance, how did she stand? She probably would take anything she could get, but just thought I was too simple. But, damn it, we sure weren't in any ballroom but in the forest, where a man is a man and not a student or an owner of an entailed estate or even a wallflower.

My old statare's hate for all upper-class children returned; I remembered how as a ten-year-old I hid behind the park trees and threw rocks at the landowner's kids just because I wasn't one of them. Later on, when they went to schools in the city to learn languages, botany, and other things which seemed to me angelic food, I borrowed an old Latin volume out of jealousy and drummed into my head hundreds of scholarly names for animals and plants.

I became still more bitter in my soul; I picked a water avens and held it up in front of the girl's nose. "With your great education surely you can tell me the Latin name for this."

Surprised, the girl let her brown eyes waver between the flower and me. "No, wha . . . what do you mean? Do you think I can remember that?"

The water avens hung its head sorrowfully and I regretted having torn it off.

"*Geum rivale*."

"That's right. Yes, of course, that's right. So what?"

She didn't sound surprised that I, a statare's kid, knew what the flower was called. Deep down, I had wanted to show off, something that always backfired when I tried calculating the effect.

"Yes, well, I just mean that if any statare's kids had had your opportunity to learn, they would have gone farther than you. Upperclass children as a rule are thickheaded."

The girl stiffened again. "You're just not very polite. Well, I really can't expect much better from you. In any event, I've done what my friend asked me to."

"Yes, you've done that and a little more besides."

"What do you mean?"

"Well, you've walked with me to the forest exactly as your friend usually does."

We were pretty far into the forest now. The girl looked around, wrinkling her black eyebrows, but the young spruce trees and junipers stayed calmly in place. "Show me the nearest way home," she ordered. "You have to be home at eleven o'clock yourself, as far as that goes."

"Oh, yes? Why do I have to do that? You're much more beautiful than your friend. She can just hang around the window until I come."

"For being an ordinary farm hand, I must say you have first-rate impudence," she said derisively.

"Thanks. From your compliment it's clear you think impudence is reserved for your social class alone."

The girl shot a look at me that in a real novel would be called "crushing" and started walking into the forest. She walked completely in the wrong direction, but it naturally didn't occur to me to suspect her of doing it on purpose.

When she had walked a little way, I hunted up a good, big rock and slung it high over her head so that it fell down in the dark bushes in front of her with a real rustle. She stopped, clutched her heart, and came back with uncertain steps while she looked around ceaselessly. "There was something horrible in there," she said, standing next to me again with a completely changed voice. "There was such an awful commotion in the bushes."

"Probably a badger, *Melus taxus*,"[1] I said gravely. "They're not too safe now that they have young ones. Lucky you turned around."

The girl stood quietly for a moment and then I heard her almost sobbing. She turned away, sulking like a school girl. My chest tightened with compassion, and I swallowed for a minute before I could say, "Oh, little one, there's no danger; besides, I'm here, no matter what."

"Yes, but you're so mean," the girl sobbed. "You're not walking out of the forest with me."

But I did. I took her hand and almost ran with her towards the edge of the forest. Now I believed in those man-eating badgers too and imagined myself in a battle with them to save the girl from their jaws. If I fell in battle against them, she'd mourn for me for a long time. While I was thinking this, we ran towards the edge of the forest.

We stopped behind some bushes there and waited while a crofter walked through the squeaking gate and past us with heavy boot steps. He walked so close we sensed the odor of the hut on his clothes. I held the girl's hand while we stood there and she didn't pull it away from me.

I felt I had to malign the thin girl, who at that moment was probably striking an interesting pose in the window. Maybe it was some way of getting closer to her friend and companion. "Naturally I wouldn't think of saying anything bad about someone who isn't here," I began, "but your friend and I can never really mean anything to each other. She takes everything so lightly."

"She is rather shallow," the girl answered by my side. "Are there any of those nasty badgers around here?"

"No, no. Not out here at the edge of the forest." But just to make sure, I stepped to the girl's forest side so she was standing with her back to the fence. Now the monsters could not get to her

---

1. Lars's Latin is incorrect. The badger of Europe and Asia is *Meles taxus*.

except over my dead body. Since she did not pull her hand away, I took her whole arm and gently stroked it. As far as I could tell in the darkness, her brown eyes harbored milder feelings for me now.

"Yes," the girl resumed on her own, "I'm not going to say too much just in case you should keep my friend waiting tonight for nothing. Well, anyway she's only played with you."

"Has she only played with me?"

The girl nodded emphatically, tramping in the moss. I slipped my arm behind her back, and she didn't try to stop me, acting as if she hadn't noticed. She was caught up in thought.

"I shouldn't talk about it, of course, but it isn't fair of her and that's why I'm going to—she has a fiancé."

"Oh!" I responded incredulously, thinking about the cave.

"An engineer. She writes to him every week and has his picture on her table. He's really handsome."

Although I had deprived the handsome one of his birthright, I still felt a kind of rancor towards him. How could he be so dumb as to leave a girl maturing on the vine? Now he had to look at some flax that had ripened before he had sharpened his scythe.

"An engineer," I said, "is what every failing upper-class student calls himself nowadays. Or a manager, although all they manage is their time. The student factories in Uppsala and Lund spew out masses of them every year, and all of them will become fine men and have titles."

"Well, you want to be better than the other workers' sons on the farm yourself," the girl answered irritatedly. "Besides, I don't think you're a very good person; you're spiteful and envious."

Deep inside, I felt she was right and so I got angry. "If the woods were full of naked men—engineers, managers, lieutenants, and workers—and you had to take the first one that came along, what would you do then?"

"What . . . ooh—what do you mean?"

"Well, how would you know who was a fine man if they didn't have either clothes or wallets on them?"

"I really can't stand this any more," the girl said coldly, pulling her arm back. "Good night—if you have any message for my friend, I'll convey it to her."

I scoured my brain for a quotation as great as it was simple and suited to the occasion but found none. But that's how it always goes, and it's one of the reasons for my unsuccessful life. Afterwards, when it's too late, my insides swarm with all the brilliant things I could have said.

In the meantime, I didn't want the girl to go home thinking I was some ordinary lout. Then she would say bad things about me to the third girl, the small one I hadn't exchanged one word with yet. But what could I do? She obviously didn't appreciate either knowledge or originality.

But the girl left before I had gotten any message ready. It was eleven-thirty. The corncrake's chirping came from two directions, and it stopped at one point when the girl walked by but then started right up again.

Infidelity and heartache hung in the fragrant night air; every thicket called with its dark womb for some titillating sin. My chest ached like an open wound when I sensed all the lust and suffering of procreation.

When I didn't see the girl any longer, I clutched my hands together and cried out sorrowfully to God. I accused Him of dilettantism in creating me but praised Him for the heavens, the earth, and everything thrusting up out of it. In that regard, I also asked him for some clarification about those matters. What did he mean by his night, his small, fine flowers, and the earth, of which in good time I would get three shovelsful in the mouth as an answer to my questions?

The cowslips slept in the cool grass. Far away across the fields a lark sang even though it was midnight. My chest got all the heavier because of all the men who would win over other men's women that night. I saw white faces with closed eyes and gasping breath in the grass; I noticed all the fine hiding places, and I sobbed the whole way home for all the world's sin and infidelity.

On the kitchen table was a letter, intent on calling me back to everyday life and its dirty perils. A soiled envelope, lined with red paper, emanating threats and unpleasantness.

Your not ansering. Maybe you think you can get out of it. But it wont work now see the dam men got to go along and its only rite. its ben six sevne months now. I got to quit my jobb soon. then you got to come across with somthing, but yor not to fine to anser my letter ill tell you. I got the law on my side, thats what somebody who knows says.

As ever,
Hilma Andersson

Now I finally decided to send off a little reminder to the woman about those five men. "Thou hast had five husbands," said Jesus, and so was I to say.

"What are those letters you're getting?" asked Mother before I even had time to get out of bed in the morning.

"Ah, shoot, it was a girl I worked with at the factory."

"Is she a nice person then?"

"Who the hell knows?"

"You aren't that kind of a friend with her, are you?" Mother asked anxiously with a mother's infernal instinct.

"No, of course not. We were just friends and I don't give a damn about her."

"That's right," said my father, attacking his oatmeal. "The kids who are never born have it the best. What's the meaning in walking around here and being nasty for fifty or sixty years? The earth has been here for fifty million years."

"You certainly don't know that," Mother answered.

"Oh yes, better than you. Primary rocks show . . . ."

"If she's a nice girl, then you could just as well stick with her as trot after the rich girls that you probably won't get anything from anyway," Mother went on.

"I don't care about either one of them," I answered.

". . . and even the different layers of the earth's crust, those great expanses of time lying behind us," Father continued.

"What are you doing out night after night if you don't care about girls? Pretty soon you're going to go do something crazy," said my mother.

"What's crazy or not," my father interjected, letting the spoonfuls of porridge disappear into his black beard, "you only see first after long stretches of time. If you're a solitary and strong human being, then everything you do seems crazy to others. You bet it does. The cows over there in the barn start mooing and making noise when a stranger comes by. The cows are like people and I'm like the stranger."

"You and your strangeness," said Mother.

"Neither my words nor your talk will keep the boy from doing stupid things. He does what he has to because of what he is. Yes, that's right. Anyway, I don't give a damn about it."

Father pushed the plate away, opened the old book with its red cover, and for the thousandth time read about the method that Stone Age man used for capturing a mammoth.

Fruit trees and blackthorn bloomed white and pink next to the huts, and down by the shore grew blue forget-me-nots. The smallest of the three girls walked picking them one Sunday morning; she walked all the way to the grass tufts and stepped out onto them. I stood farther up among the bird cherries, which had just finished blooming, and I felt a wondrous yearning in my heart when I saw that girl. The church bells rang serenely, and the morning was warm and calm.

Everything was unchanged down here since I had tended the cows as a seven-year-old. The church bells had rung then too and I thought with pleasure—now it's eleven o'clock. Then I approvingly counted how many of the cows lay down and swore about the greediness of the others that still walked munching in the grass and reeds.

Then there was one day—let me see—six years ago. Calm and late summer, the reeds and sedge had brown spots from the frost. The water was very clear and some small fish swam slowly away from the shore when I came. Sometimes they bumped their snouts against a reed, making it quiver. On the bottom, peculiar little creatures moved, gray and pentangular. You could imagine that a child had busied himself cutting them out of gray paper.

Tiny, tiny bugs rose hastily to the surface, stopped for a second, then returned to the protective forest of decaying plant matter on the bottom. The summer's last dragonflies, blue as beryls, flew slowly, rustling their wings over the motionless reeds. If you stood still, they would land on your hand and doze in the unexpected warmth, turning their heads on their narrow necks as if in sleep.

The girl stepped on the tufts of grass, occasionally putting her hand above her eyes and looking out over the cove. I looked at her and thought that neither the slender girl nor the brown-eyed girl would go so well together with sun, Sunday, tussocks, and cove. I had no intention of showing myself or talking to her, even though I had my best suit on.

She walked by so close to me that I could see her little turned-up nose and those blue eyes that even now smiled over at something in the distance. Her legs bent a bit outwards, but that didn't matter. All the same, I wondered how it could have happened. She probably had had rachitis as a child, and because her parents came from the upper class, they couldn't let themselves trust Madam Hägglöf's rickets salve. That ointment had made my legs and my brother's and sister's legs straight and strong, which my mother did not fail to point out often.

The smoke rose blue from the chimneys, and I realized that statare women were preparing that liquid known as morning coffee. At our place, that consisted of black chicory water for everyday use; the coffee grinder solemnly clattered only on Sundays.

When the children were small, Mother baked hard-bread biscuits for the coffee from time to time. She made some dough and rolled out long strips from it, cut off half-inch bits, and baked them brown. Then she burned them still more in a roasting pan together with some startled coffee beans so they would taste of coffee.

Chicory is called *intubi* and comes from the endive—*intybus*—

root. I often noticed the beautiful blue flower on the graveled roadsides and did not hold it responsible for its underground mission. The *intubi* cost five öre[1] apiece and was never absent from our house. While we were small, those black, oblong bits always bore our teeth marks; we could never convince ourselves that they weren't licorice.

I was torn between the morning coffee and the girl, who just disappeared like the dawn among the bird cherries. I finally decided to go home for coffee, especially since the pathway meandered alluringly through the grass in that direction. I was never very happy about tramping in the grass and flowers; I thought that in some way I was not worthy of stepping on that fragrant, living carpet with my more or less dirty and sweaty feet with their ugly toes.

The pathway went into a denser clump of trees and hinted with a slight opening through them where it meant to come out again. Two boys in Sunday clothes stood hitting the trunk of a spruce tree to get the crow to fly out of its nest, which sat like a pile of twigs in the top. When I walked by, one boy whispered audibly to the other, "The tall one there can almost get the crow's eggs without even climbing up." And both put their hands to their mouths.

I said nothing to the boys but took their remark as a new proof that malice is mankind's child, inbred, attending him from cradle to grave.

Mother and Father fell silent when I came in, and I knew they had been talking about me. It probably started to worry them that I didn't get a new job. I didn't make any real effort to get one either. And a six-foot, six-inch man, of course, seems much more unemployed than a little fellow, who can slip in here and there and make himself inconspicuous. I had a few indefinite plans, however, that sometime I would do something of one kind or another that was damned stupendous.

I looked at the machines in the shed and wondered if any were yet to be invented. Or if some important improvement could be made on them. A baler that cut, dried, and threshed the grain and

1. An öre is one one-hundredth of a Swedish crown. At this time, the crown was worth approximately twenty-seven cents.

let it run down into sacks which it placed on the field. The main thing was somehow to get people to talk about me and the smallest girl to admire me.

I kept an eye open in the forest just in case some natural law that had escaped mankind until then should reveal itself to me. I broke off some fool's silver from a mound of mica and wondered if it couldn't be used for something. Well—I'd get back to it some other time. I wrote it down in my notebook.

I put my ear against the trunks of the spruce trees and tried to listen to some secret from plant life, unknown to scholars and professors. I wrote for a seventy-five-öre microscope from Åhlén and Holm's Mail Order House and looked at fly wings and spider legs but found nothing that was not in the science books. I should have lived a hundred years earlier.

And the whole time the accusation from town lay in the bottom of my soul somewhere, upsetting me. Like a big croaker in a clear well, it lay waiting. I hoped anyway that the kid's entrance into the world would prove my innocence since I had had the honor of meeting Hilma Andersson only one time. But my hate for those two nasty letters was great.

The old man came along the road from the forest and his white beard shone from far off. Before we met, he sat down on a rock lying by the side of the road. It was a good rock to sit on, and he was taking some snuff contentedly when I sat down in the ditch beside him.

"The forest has grown like hell," he said. "I've been out looking at it. I remember when there was just marsh out there; you had to do with the biggest sapling for a Christmas tree. And now it's real timber, all of it."

But I was having one of my darker days and answered with wise and bitter words: "Yes, but so what? The owner sells the timber and gets a few thousand crowns for it, and then the devil takes him. His kids divide the wealth he leaves behind, fight about it and kick it around. Then it's gone, all of it."

"You know, from here you could see the mountain lying right inside the forest before the forest grew up," the old man responded. "On Walpurgis Night, we built bonfires on the highest point. If you look, you can see that the mountain's scorched from the heat."

I lay in the ditch, looking up at the old man. Strange that he wasn't afraid, he who could not live much longer. He looked out over the field, and his eyes were alert. If only I could understand.

"What did you say about the master?" he asked.

"Nothing. But look at this dandelion. It'll wither away soon, but it can do that calmly, of course; next spring it'll come up again. From the same root. But when I'm buried, I'll never come up again."

"It probably doesn't matter."

"Yes, but what if there's another life after this one as some believe? A heaven?"

"Then let there be. I'll get there without going to the chapel and making a lot of fuss. I've worked my whole life and I've provided for those I've brought into the world. If God doesn't count such things, then he's a poor master. But you shouldn't think about things like that, young man. Why do you do it?"

"Can't help it."

"You can go crazy. Though it'll probably pass when you get older and have a family. Such thoughts don't work out so well in a statare's hut, believe me. There you have to work every day till you're dead tired, and every night listen to the wife's whining and the kids' bawling."

He did not want to understand me, and I decided to give it to him, terrify him but good.

"For eighty-five years you've walked around here seeing the sun, the earth, and everything that grows and blooms. But any day now you'll go down in the earth, deep under the tree roots. Someone else will move into your cabin and sit in the sunshine by the window. After a few years, no one will remember that you ever existed, even though you'd lived such a long time. The groundskeeper makes the mound level with the earth when no one tends it."

40

So I said, looking up the whole time into the old man's face. I thought I'd see his old, horrified eyes wander about a moment, but they glittered gladly and peacefully towards the field.

"You sure have a lot of shit in your head," he answered me. "You read too many books. Sure I can kick the bucket any minute now, but who thinks about that? When I was younger I was in a state about it sometimes but not any more now. That's the way it is and that's it. Isn't that in your books?"

I became immensely happy. Could it be true that the pit got smaller the nearer you got to it? That there was a long and calm leveling out towards the end? But the sky clouded over again.

"I had a brother who read and talked almost like you," said the old man. "That is, there weren't so many books at that time. But he wanted to be a little better than his brother and sisters too."

"Didn't he do it then?"

"He died—when was it now—'65 in the autumn. He was dead without being sick. It was probably just as well, since he never did want to do anything useful."

"How old was he?"

"Oh, he must have been about twenty-five."

God, I thought, my lips turning dry, just like me this year. My heart beat painfully against my ribs, and I thought that the grave opened before me in the clover. The old man said something about how the rye looked promising when I got up and left to rescue myself with the help of my body's mechanical movements. From the beginning of time it was probably ordained that just at that moment a blue-white cloud would block the sun and a cool breeze would move from east to west.

It was getting close to twelve and the drivers came home in a long row with their horses. The cloud's shadow went farther away over the fields, glided out into the cove, and disappeared over the ridge on the other side. I looked around; the old man was still sitting on the rock, and he turned his head in every direction. Everything was still at midday; nothing moved except the heat waves, which silently quivered against the forest's edge. Above the dry clay ditch the bindweed climbed and spread out its strange, tender flowers.

A little farther away lay two adders rolled up in the blazing hot sunshine on the ditch bank. After I watched them a while, they lifted their flat heads, flashed their tongues, and glided silently down under a little osier bush at the bottom of the ditch. Nearby, a dry snakeskin was barely visible in the grass. The buzzing of insects intensified the blazing hot melancholy of midday.

A large part of the forest had been felled the preceding winter and the timber taken away. The branches lay behind, a meter thick, all twisted together. The landowner offered to let me trim them and lay them in meter-high piles. He said it was a shame not to have anything to do, big and tall as I was. He offered me wretchedly little pay, which, on the other hand, was only fitting and not a shame at all.

I went over there, watching a day warmed by the sun. Father, who hoped I would start with the twigs, had already sharpened a broken scythe for me to trim with. He had wrapped a rag where I was going to hold it so I wouldn't get blisters on my hands.

Millions of angry wood ants crawled on the branches, and I had to stamp continuously to get them to roll off my legs, which they tirelessly assaulted. Where the branches lay thinner, grass, nettles, and strawberry blossoms stuck through. Large mossy stones, which had slumbered under the spruce trees for a thousand years, now found themselves exposed to the sun and the winds.

I felt almost physical revulsion for assaulting the vast field of spruce twigs with my sickle. If I refused, the judgment, which was being whispered already, would be said out loud—"lazy, incompetent, vain."

I stamped the ants off and went into the large, humming forest. For several hours I walked, trying to find some way to live. But everything was futile; there was no task for me in the whole boundless world other than this mass of spruce twigs.

The sickle lay on the steps and glowered reproachfully at me when I came home. I said inside: "Good, damn the whole thing, sackcloth handle and all." In the hut, Father had dug out an old glove that would keep my left hand from being torn by the twigs.

The next morning Mother filled a thermos bottle with coffee and laid it and three slices of wheat bread and some sugar cubes in a basket. Father mentioned something about how you ought to turn all the twigs in the same direction so the whole thing would look better. Both looked pleased, but my chest felt like I had just swallowed a hedgehog. I had to force my legs forward every step towards the forest. I met several crofters walking to the farm, and they grinned knowingly when they saw the coffee basket and sickle as if they thought, "Oh yes, you, you devil." I was furious at them for their ability to work so naturally. But, of course, they could not know how much I hated tools, work clothes, and regular hours.

Nothing was wrong with the morning; as usual, it was a pleasant mixture of warmth from the sun and a lingering coolness from the night. The dew beaded on the spider webs among the twigs. I walked past a huge anthill, and then I remembered that someone had once spoken a word of wisdom that could apply to me: "Go to the ants and learn."

I put the basket on a stump and began studying the ants. It was like a brown, crawling fell, all of it, and when I held my hand a yard above the hill, thousands of fine streams sprayed up against it from the ants' natural artillery. I thought that the ants waged war as men did, though without such devilish equipment. If I had anything to say in the world, I would say to the warlike, "Go to the ants and learn. Fight with the equipment the Creator supplied you with. Piss on each other."

I did not learn a thing from that seemingly purposeless crawling mass of ants. True, I did see a few ants in the grass struggling towards their pyramid with a berry, a dead fly, or a dry larva in their jaws. And from them, of course, I should learn to drag my straw to my hill, to serve the pyramid fatherland. But why hasn't anyone found out which straw was suited for me to bear? One that I could bear without agony.

The church dean's son had fists like sledgehammers, and he wanted to grub in the earth and chop timber; he preferred a leather jersey to a tennis shirt, but he was forced to be in Uppsala holding books in his mighty fists. I who bitterly envied him his white student cap,[1] I was put to cleaning up the ravaged forest. Let him and me trade places, you meddlesome anthill, in which I'm an unhappy ant.

I gave up the anthill and walked up a mountain that had previously been hidden by the forest. A cairn from the Bronze Age lay in the middle of the mountain in a circle. I thought about those men who, three thousand years ago, had dragged the stones together over the body of their dead friend or lord. They wanted the dead one not to be forgotten, and you could say that they had achieved their goal. After three thousand years, a being sat on his barrow thinking about him. Would the modern, lovely gravestones last as long, I wondered?

So a kind of shameful burning in my chest told me I should start working. "In a minute," I answered and thought on.

When there were only a few people in the forests and on the shores, life was big and simple in them. Everything they did was strong and firm. The caves, the graves, and the weapons. But their hearts were tender and reliable. Now everything was just the opposite. Now there are many more of us and we produce nothing but crap and glitter. Except for deadly weapons, of course; they are made with greater care than ever before.

Man was simple and strong then; now he's wandering and clever. He calls it science and has infused it into all the daily functions of his life. The nightly ones too. Modern man puts away his cigarette and sleeps with his woman, freshly shaved, pale, and small-boned, and probably thinks about an affair while he avoids conception through science.

So I thought instead of trimming twigs, which was proper for a worker and a worker's son. My conscience, or whatever the hell it was, gave me a new stinging lash across some kind of interior be-

1. Students attending the university in Uppsala, founded in 1477, and other Swedish universities traditionally wear white caps, signifying that they have matriculated.

hind. I looked at the coffee basket and decided to drink the coffee before I started the work. The decision brought me temporary relief.

The brown, miniature people had found their way into the basket and sat fast on the sugar cubes. When I wanted to take the cubes, they set themselves against me, disregarding any property rights. No poor devil is sent to the ants to learn about that. I discovered all by myself that the Japanese are an ant people—small, brown, and fiery. Just flood over and start in on someone else's property. Created to haul for their thoughtless master, fight, and die. Be scattered out on the ground and become one with it.

After coffee, there was no more avoiding it. I put on my glove, gripped the sickle, which was burning hot from the sun, and beheld once more the twig field's hell of needles. Down towards the cove some seedling spruces remained and cast out a little shadow. I saw it and immediately decided to start down there. There were probably fewer ants down there too.

It took a good while to get there through the rugged terrain, and I had to sit on a stump there and rest. It was not many yards from the lake; there were small waves on it and tender reeds stuck up in clumps. Occasionally a fish splashed next to a clump. I sat there missing my boyhood fishing rod.

I must admit, thinking of those three girls, I was also ashamed for having to take that work. I wanted them to think me big and brilliant enough not to need to work with my hands. Furthermore, I wanted them to think me one who, one beautiful day, could come up with a real surprise. People would have occasion to say, "Who could believe that about him?"

Now it seemed like the natural thing to do was to invent a machine that could trim all those twigs, to take out a patent on it, and then become rich and famous. The thought greatly pleased me, and I decided to lie in the grass while I mulled it over. You think better when you're lying down. And besides, I didn't need to have any pangs of conscience when the thought had to do with the work at hand. Thought comes before all action.

It may have been the soothing wind's and buzzing insects' fault that I dozed off. The waves probably helped out too with their whispering in the grass by the shore. My noble intent when I lay down in the grass was to make life for the labor-burdened segment of humanity more tolerable with my invention.

When I awoke, everything was quiet; the cove lay calm and the sun burned hot. The statare whom I had seen far in the distance had disappeared with their horses, and I realized that it was midday.

My chest got colossally heavy when I thought that my parents sat eating dinner, but I was not worthy to sit with them at the table. He who will not work and so on. I realized it was something fundamentally wrong with me, that great repulsion for work. I cried over my awkwardness right in the midst of warm, rich nature, and when an ant went by with a needle in its jaws, I flicked it and sent it flying.

If I could only get in touch with whatever must be behind, whatever I intimated was beyond everything. I clutched my hands together but felt ashamed and took them apart again; if there was anyone who heard, I would talk to him directly and without ceremony, "If you're there and hear me," I said right out into the air, "then I have to ask you to show me the way a little. This is like hell. Surely you can show me how to start at least. True, I'm a poor, insignificant thing, but as long as I exist, I have to bet on myself. Now show me how I should start, but do it fast."

A mild breeze caressed my face, and I took it as a sign. A lofty thought quickly made itself felt, kicking out the teeming rubbish so that it alone remained.

"You shall start where you stand," said the thought. "If you're standing amongst twigs, then why the deuce not start with that? Afterwards, you'll see the next step for sure."

"I haven't had any dinner," I tried to object. But the thought said that because I had snoozed the whole morning, I didn't need anything yet.

Now I thought that a pair of large, calm eyes observed me from someplace, and it was a wholesome fancy. I wanted to be on their good side, of course, and I have sensed them looking at me many times since then. I told an old religious woman about them, and she thanked God and wanted to have me come to the chapel. But I told her to go to hell.

She believed that it was their chapel God, smelling of coffee and saffron, who looked at me in the forest. He who terrified my days and nights when I was a child and was forced to attend that morbid, dirty trick against delicate souls that's called Sunday school. Very early I was stuffed full of horrible details from a dissipated, past people's way of life. But I told the old woman to go to the devil.

Because someone standing silent in the forest watched me, I was immediately proud and felt in some way chosen. And, of course, I could very well trim away a few twigs; soon I would be lifted above all demeaning physical labor.

Consequently some stacks of twigs grew up under my hands, and when the evening sun lengthened the spruce trees' shadows halfway out into the cove, I walked home to Mother, who in a worried tone objected to my foolishly going the whole day without any food.

I ran into those three girls now and then; they were sun-tanned and didn't have much on in the warmth. The two I knew responded coolly and with dignity to my greeting, and I saw that they had agreed I was a louse. The tiny one smiled a little one day and sent a little blue sparkle right into my eyes. I was happy for two days, and the sickle flew like a lark's wing.

We bought a liter of three-star cognac for Midsummer's Eve, a crofter's boy my own age and I. We went to the paint store and bought some pieces of violet root to chew on, too, so our breath wouldn't smell like liquor. We drank from the liter in the brush above the maypole, and we were as happy as calves. Just as dumb, too. We shook hands on sticking together whatever might happen and then went down to the field where some skinny confirmation class girls had already started hopping around the pole.

A little school girl came up to me with a message from the

brown-eyed girl. She was in such and such a place, and she wanted to say a few words to me.

I gave the school kid ten öre and walked away while the cognac reeled merrily in my head and my friend sent a guffaw and a shameful suggestion after me. But I thought it was only natural that she should send for me—on Midsummer's Eve only happy things could happen.

The girl walked among the bird cherries, and her spider web of a dress fit superbly. You couldn't mistake a single detail of her body's outline. I spit out the violet root and bowed a little stiffly. We had quarreled, after all, the last time we met.

The girl was a little rigid, too, and from the beginning she wanted to emphasize that she did not want anything from me for her part. She thought about her friend now too. The problem was that her fiancé, the engineer, had arrived and would soon be coming down to the maypole with her. Now the brown-eyed one wanted to prepare me and assure herself that I would not do anything rash out of jealousy. She had heard that I flared up easily.

After I explained that her slender friend could, for all I cared, have ten engineers and just as many managers, I tried to take hold of the brown-eyed's overflow but immediately got a sock in the nose. Then I went down to the field again and sorrowfully told everything to my drinking buddy. We decided to let the engineer live for the time being and limit ourselves to workers' daughters. We hoped, however, that for his own good he wouldn't seem stuck-up.

At dinner a few hours earlier, my father, who'd taken a few giant snorts said, "Tonight, Midsummer's Eve, the bracken blooms. The one who can sneak up there and take a look gets whatever he wishes for. You can bet the deuce on that!"

"Ah, sure."

"Goddamn it. It's Old Nick himself sitting out there in the bush, and it looks like it's going to burn up when it blooms. My father saw it himself."

"What did he wish for then?"

"He was drunk and forgot to make a wish before it was too late. He told me about it, but I've never gotten around to going."

"You have the same problem your father did," Mother observed. "You're drunk every Midsummer's Eve. Besides, you shouldn't joke about something secret. It can just as well be left alone."

I thought about that conversation a little later when I stood by the maypole and watched the people wobbling and stalking around to a furiously screeching accordion. The smallest of those three girls stood by herself for a moment, and the cognac gave my soul courage to go and talk with her. I forgot to make myself interesting and didn't talk about the Ice Age, Mira, or the flowers. It felt like a holy day for me to get to stand next to her, although she was simply dressed compared to her two friends.

I don't know what I said to the girl, but the humbleness and thankfulness of my heart made my speech simple and direct. When I told her the legend of the bracken that bloomed, she suggested herself that we should go and look at it when it got near twelve o'clock. Now we should part so no one would see that we left together later.

So the girl said and looked bluely right inside me. I went up on the forest slope so that no one would see how beastly glad I was. Meanwhile, by force of habit, I began running myself down but failed in everything significant. I made a respectable try anyway and called myself stupid and stuck-up, but nothing penetrated my depths. They were filled with a clear light.

Now with some old and tried patterns, I ought to be able to tell how full of feeling our walking off at midnight was, how the forest stood silent and the flowers gave off their scent. All of that probably happened, but I didn't think any more about it. But when we came to a gate, I felt a wild urge to do something unusual, and so I found myself flying towards the gate, bent on taking a huge jump over it. Naturally my shinbones hit the top wood slate and I dove over the gate onto my head and down into the cow pen where the cows had been standing close together. No one could blame them for standing close together, and I got my hands and knees full of cow shit and mud.

The girl came through the gate fast, her face full of anxiety and surprise. She did not laugh, and for that I hope she gets eternal bliss one day.

"You idiot," she said gently, "what came over you?"

She snatched off some grass and helped me brush off the knees of my serge suit. I washed myself in a marsh and got a little fragrant handkerchief from her to wipe my hands with. I, a long-legged and smeared figure of misery, got her little handkerchief, and she helped me fix up my trouser legs even though she wasn't any taller than either one of them. She was like a little, gentle mother, and I felt a wild craving to be allowed to protect her from something dangerous.

We sat on a knoll among live-forevers, stonecrops, and water arum. We kept watch over some bracken bushes in front of us, and I explained to the girl that bracken bushes are higher and denser than other ferns. Those who come from upper-class schools don't know much. The girl had heard that I had a good head, and she thought that I would eventually become something. I listened with inner jubilation and decided to become something damned important.

She, of course, had breasts, legs, and something more besides, this girl too, but I didn't think about that for a second. We were alone, it was midnight and dark in the forest, but I was as free from temptation as if I were standing outside one winter night in just a shirt looking at the stars. And even so, my whole body, whose house guest—if it had any—was spiritual, screamed loudly for her. I wanted to take her, carry her a little ways, and set her down again. I wanted much more besides that there aren't any words for.

And at the same time everything was so simple. I was not at all surprised when she suddenly put out her little hand for me to hold.

While we sat like that, the black and the white inside me barked at each other like two dogs. The white regretted all the filth, all the love that had taken place behind the bushes, and suggested how beautiful a little purity would have been just now. But the black dog stood his ground, thinking that I was a wretch who believed someone else was better and that I should instead immediately become the biggest swine in creation. He barked something else about how maybe the little fist I held had done exciting and daring experiments in the darkness of the bedroom.

The devil did not appear, at least not visibly, and I felt almost like an impostor in front of the girl. I rationalized by thinking that all natural mystique had died, all secret things had withdrawn, because of people's increasing superficiality and mechanization. I blended together one cup Emerson and two cups Schopenhauer and firmly believed that it was my own words that poured out. Many of my successes with upper-class women have depended on their never having read heavy things and therefore believing that they had discovered a genius where there was only a phonograph.

It grew lighter and the spots on my trousers stood out more clearly. And obviously, of course, the birds chirped, the dew fell, and a flotilla of two white and six gray swans swam on the shiny black cove. All that had been going on for thousands of years, and, goddamn it, there sure wasn't any reason to stop it that night.

Out on the field, the accordion grew silent with a last distressful cry. We heard voices and laughter from those walking home in a flock, the confirmation group who played at being big and experienced but who still didn't dare crawl off to the side and lie down. They guided their bicycles bought on credit and raised unjustified whoops when the sun came up.

Just below where we were sitting was a walking path and on it came two brothers who lived in the forest district and were cycling home. The younger one rode a woman's bicycle with a simple gear system and pedaled ardently without seeing us.

"Yes, now this Midsummer Eve's gone," he said when they were right in front of us.

"Yeah, to hell with it," the other one answered morosely without turning around. With legs cranking, both vanished behind the young spruce trees.

We sat for an hour more, not saying very much. The crofter's cows came up from the large forest and went down to the shore to drink, and their bells rang serenely. Their muzzles floated on the water between water lily leaves, and their large eyes looked at us indifferently. Their tails fanned at the horseflies, which were already at work, and the smell of animals and mud reached us when they stepped in the sludge along the shore.

I got a squeeze from the little hand when we parted, and that made me feel rich for several days. We didn't need to arrange a meeting; we sensed we were going to meet again anyway.

On the way home, I thought that now I really had to take myself in hand in order to deserve my success somehow. The girl had come to me even though I was nothing, and one day she was going to see she hadn't made a mistake. For a few more days I would trim branches until my plans had taken firmer shape.

Father sat sleeping with his head on the table when I came into the cabin and I knew he had been good and drunk. The flies played on the table and crawled on his big hands, which he had laid in front of him. Buzzing, they mated zealously on *The Wonder of the Universe* as if they had seen some sign threatening a declining birthrate.

"Can't you get some life into your father?" Mother's voice complained from the bedroom. "He's just sitting there getting completely stiff."

But I let him sit; he mumbled and swore in his sleep and I knew he wasn't so bad off. With a new shimmer in the junkyard of my soul, I crept down on my bench where the cat yawned and stretched out its paws.

But Midsummer's Day threw a monkey wrench into the works. Another letter with wobbly style. The threats were sharper now. "I have talked with those who know the law and damn you if you don't answer. The time's right too so don't try it. I'm so big I can't even go to the movies. If, my idiot, I'd only tried to get rid of it before it was too late. You'll probably be cocky enough when the child welfare committee gets a hold of you. As ever . . . ."

The beautiful day turned into an autumn day in the shadow of Hilma Andersson and the child welfare committee. I swore horrible streaks about my persecution and at the same time felt a creeping anxiety eating at me from the inside.

I took the letter out with me, and on the other side of the fruit trees I tore it into small bits, which I scattered out over the currant bushes. Then I walked along the ditch banks far out across the fields, but the letter had put me beyond the wild strawberry flowers and the hum of the insects, and inside me rolled a lump of dough made of shame and filth. I washed my hands demonstratively in the stream rippling in the high grass.

If the girl hears about it, I thought where I squatted by the stream, if she hears that I've been singled out as father to hotel dishwasher Hilma Andersson's first-born son . . . .

"Then I'll jump in here," I said out loud, without thinking that the stream was just half a meter deep.

If I had looked around when I tore the letter into bits, I would have seen a big spiteful old bitch's mug parting the raspberry bushes and staring at me. If I had looked back when I had walked a bit, I would have seen the spying mug's owner, the coachman's housekeeper, swaying forward and carefully gathering together all the pieces of the letter. Had I then been able to look into the coachman's dark kitchen, I would have seen her, kindly assisted by her master and coachman, fitting the pieces together and pasting them onto a piece of paper so you could read the letter. When the work was done, I would have seen those two old people beaming with pleasure at the thought of being able to persecute and torment a younger and therefore enviable fellow human being.

Suddenly I met Hilma Andersson's father, and it seemed he had seen me from a distance and deliberately tried to run into me. He was an old man with a red-gray beard, and he used to read the Bible and go to chapel. Consequently he was crafty and sly and you never knew where he stood. Now when I saw him coming, I wondered if he knew anything about his daughter's advanced condition.

"Oh, so you're not messing around with the branches today," he said, whinnying.

"I damned well shouldn't have to work on Midsummer's Day any more than anyone else."

"No, of course not. But maybe because you might need . . . some income. Ha, ha."

And he glowered at me with a kind of cowardly, grinning anger. I realized he knew everything.

"No matter how big an income I have, I'm not going to support other people's bastards," I blurted out, continuing on my way, breathless with emotion. There, he got something to chew on that made his beard bob up and down. Damned old man! Fur coat Jesus! And the like would come to every single one who didn't have better sense than to take me on.

But my new happiness quickly laid its hand on the waves and, you see, they grew completely calm. A little figure sat fast on my retina, and I soon surprised myself by walking with the corners of my mouth near my ears when I thought of her. I sat on a ditch bank and took out my notebook. Among quotes from Nietzsche, Emerson, and many another great precursor's work, I wrote my rhymed, flat-footed verses. Then I walked home and so that was Midsummer.

Driven by some unexplainable impulse, the girl started loving me. There was no mistaking it. I recognized all the usual symptoms; not one was missing. On the contrary, some new ones came along with them. I talked with her somberly about how we must part since she stood so high above me, and simultaneously thought with horror that she could take me at my word. But she wouldn't go along with it but instead humbled herself before me, and once she even kissed my hand. My big veined fist. Can you imagine that?

It was in the middle of haying season when we realized what there was between us. We walked into the meadow barn and sat down in the new hay. She didn't let me draw her into the barn giggling affectedly like the other girls. Instead she walked in openly and looked for a place where we could sit. The sun was going down. It shone in through the broad slits and the opened door. From the ceiling high above us hung huge, dusty spider webs, swaying slowly.

The girl didn't say much, but her eyes were glued to me and I saw their blue, boundless affection. And again I forgot the woman and only saw a tiny girl who I wanted to give my life for. I stroked her hair as tenderly as I could and saw her eyes fill with tears without her turning them from me.

Here, naturally, I should have taken her in my arms, experienced fellow that I was, but I sat mute and foolish. None of my earlier tricks seemed to fit here.

Later when we lay in the hay and she pressed her school-girl body against me, I thought that she did not know about doing anything beyond that. Compared to both her friends, she left me almost untouched. I wondered what there was about this little creature that was so desirable if it wasn't her body. Body and woman had been the same thing for me until then. I had chosen to impress both the other girls to get them to lose their balance in a barn or a bush, but the one here who freely crept next to me in the hay I could not touch in any way other than a father would, stroking his child.

A powerful feeling of ownership filled me completely when I held that little body in my arms. At the start, I imagined that feeling, like many other reasonable sensations, was typical for me alone, but since then, I have noticed with surprise that almost every person I've met has felt the same way. I became more and more convinced that I was a normal human being. Almost every guy or girl has come out with a similar hay barn or bush idyll when I, my voice quivering with emotion, have told mine.

Nowadays I can say "I" without enthusiasm in my voice, but then I studied my own sensations respectfully and marvelingly and counted them singular and brilliant.

Each and every impulse terrified me with its violent and transitory nature. Like the one I felt here in the barn where we sat the first night. I wasn't drunk, and besides that, I was a normal human being.

When all the hay was taken in, the barn doors were locked, but they sat so high that you could crawl under them if you lay on your stomach. We came hand in hand, wanting to be someplace where no one could see our almost always quiet happiness. The July night was silent and tired around us. We both looked in under the barn door and then I crawled in first. When I got up inside in the dark, her head stuck in like the dawn under the door, and then a terrible power whispered to me to kick her in the head.

I drew my leg back, but then reason returned and I turned rigid with horror. What a terrible beast I was! I had read a lot about mental aberration and now I thought it was finished. My diaphragm trembled for several hours, causing the girl to wonder and worry.

Another time, I clutched her in my arms until she turned blue-white in the face and shut her eyes. But she did not scream; instead she became even more tender towards me when she came to again.

The highest beams became softly gilded in the sunset, and big, cheerful flies fought for the best places in the sun. A forgotten lunch pail with its coffee thermos hung on a nail and we were a little anxious that its owner would come back to get it. But soon it grew dark in the barn and the bats flew past the door with abrupt turns as they began hunting mosquitoes. A cool breeze came in through the door. I put hay over the girl's legs and silk stockings and tried to find her mouth in the dimness.

I didn't miss my notebook until afternoon the next day. I thought about where I could have lost it and realized it must be in the barn from the night before. I had better go and look. My cheeks flushed hot when I thought that someone could have found it and read my thoughts about life, women, and other mystifications. I tossed away the glove and sickle, brushed off the ants, and set off for the barn, which glimmered red far off among the birch trees.

Then I saw the hayload creep up towards the barn. Damn it! If they drove hay in there today, the book would be either discovered or buried under the hay.

I approached the barn from the rear and got there just at the coffee break. Already at a distance, I heard bursts of laughter coming in unison from different voices, ranging from the head farm hand's bass to the youngest boy's breaking treble. Angry and ashamed, I sneaked next to the barn wall and listened. Yes, that was right. Through an opening I could see the happy discoverer

sitting in the hay with the notebook in his rough claws, surrounded by the others. Important and often interrupted by his
own snorting laughter, he spelled out some words and read the
others.

He read great words from Nietzsche, sharp diatribes from
Schopenhauer, and beautiful verses from me without differentiating them, and the others laughed the whole time just to make
sure. I despised those cruel animals from where I stood outside
the wall. My strength, my consolation and Bible, the notebook,
they whinnied at, "ha ha" and "ho ho." The feeling of standing
alone outside those two large classes of people came strongly over
me again, and I turned around without getting the book back.
The whole time I thought that something black was coming from
behind me, looking for an opportunity to dig in.

I got the book back that night. The discoverer had given it to
my father with a grin and a guess that pretty soon I'd probably
forget the girl behind in the hay too. Father, seeing my distress,
tried to improve my mood with an example from mankind's
history.

"Don't you think that Cro-Magnon man had his problems with
women too?" he asked. "Stone Age man fought with his hand
wedges about women and caves, and now in modern times you're
blubbering because you don't get to lie in peace with the woman
you want. Don't you understand that it doesn't mean anything?"

"Lie in peace! That isn't it at all."

"Oh, yes, it is. Everything boils down to that. Even though
your youth dresses the whole thing up so you can think your case
is special and grand. But it damn well isn't. You feel you're big and
noble, but all your feelings come from your pants. You can believe
that."

"Then that's why you never find any good feelings in people
who've quit . . . whatever you mean with the pants."

"You ought to read *The Wonder of the Universe*," Father said, a
little annoyed. "If you take good care of it. You can see there how
most things are. And then you can get a little truer view about
your own dimensions compared with the universe. There was a
kind of land crocodile once five hundred times bigger than you

are. It ate treetops. What do you mean—and the girl, the barn, the men, and me too as far as that goes? Not more than fly shit. You can find the crocodile on page 215 in the book."

July's long, hot days left me in peace, and I started hoping that the hotel dishwasher had begun to treat one of the other five men to her writings. Of course I felt a heavy, threatening calm in the air, but I still did not know where the wind would start blowing. While waiting for it, I got what I could from the days and nights; my heart ached with longing for the tiny girl until we managed in the evenings to sneak past evil, glistening eyes in the cabin windows, getting away to satisfy ourselves with each other.

More and more, I noticed an anxiety growing in that girl's body; sometimes she pressed it against me in a way I recognized from others. It hurt me and I reproached her in the mildest terms my mouth could form. But she gasped, pressed herself still hotter against me, and said plaintively, "Hit me, I'm a beast. But it's because I love you so terribly." Inside me the fear struck that the girl would consider me a poor lover, bent on keeping our relationship clean and pure. But of course I suspected that it would mature in one way or the other.

Some flies, drowsy at midday but obstinate, were witnesses to a warm Sunday afternoon's coupling of the shaggy-black-haired and the little blonde-haired pair in the forest. The spruces hid some whimpering breaths and the sun dried some tears on a pair of tender girl's cheeks. The moss discretely hid some drops of blood, and when I went and looked at the place the next day, the cat's-feet had risen again.

"Your father and chimney sweep Sundvall have gone to catch crayfish," my mother said one evening in the beginning of August. "And you got a letter again."

I swore silently about the letter but said aloud, "Let it be until I get back. I'm going down to watch the old men."

The chimney sweep and my father walked along the stream bank with pants legs rolled up. In the grass at the edge of the stream stood a half-empty liter bottle. The two old men groped about on the bottom and accompanied each catch with a loud yell.

"A crayfish," screamed the chimney sweep, holding the object he yelled about in the air. "A big devil. We'll have a drink on that."

The old men waded to shore, looked indifferently at me, and sat down by the bottle. They marked it with their thumbnails before turning the bottom towards the Lord. Swore, laughed, and bragged. With their naked arms, legs, and feet, they looked like some kind of strange prehistoric creatures that had come up out of the water to taste liquor from a later age.

When they got up, the bottle was empty and the old men more than half drunk. They grabbed hold of each other and started to perform a kind of dance of joy and friendship on the edge of the stream. Suddenly they stepped so near the brink that a strip of soil gave way, they lost their balance and rolled swearing and struggling down the slope and out into the water. There they finally let go of each other and crept snorting to shore. With wet beards hanging straight down and eyes glaring, they resembled a pair of walruses on the attack.

The summer night was warm; they got undressed and wrung the water out of their clothes. When I was through laughing, I went home. Behind me I heard their voices. The chimney sweep swore continuously over the mishap, but Father was already looking philosophically at the event.

"Didn't do any harm," said his calm voice. "What the hell? Now you got your filthy shirt washed. There's a meaning in everything. But it was a damned shame the liter went empty so quick."

This time all my Christian names were on the letter, which is the first sign that society has intervened in one's private life. Besides that, the envelope was clean and cheap, not soiled with love-red lining like Hilma Andersson's.

While I squinted with emotion, I read that I was the father of dishwasher Hilma Andersson's child, born on such and such a day, and all of whose names were also listed. Now I had to appear on a certain day in town to confer with the child welfare woman about the size of my contribution for child support. If I didn't appear, a summons would be taken out for me the same day.

I couldn't tell my parents about it; it stuck in my throat too much. But I could surely tell it to the eighty-five-year-old man who, the day after, walked striking the ditch banks with his old red scythe. I told him about it and my voice was a mixture of tears and anger. The old man sat down in the ditch and thought.

"You say you never got near her. Then for sure it's not right. Used to be that they didn't give a damn who the father of a bastard was. The girls had to go suckle them at the orphanage. It was that simple back then. The girls had to go there two or three times a day at the start so the kids could suck."

"But now it's the girls who point the finger at any man they feel like. And if he doesn't pay, damn him. He goes off to forced labor," I said heavy-heartedly.

The old man nodded and seemed to think about a way to help me.

"So it is. But can't you get a paper from the factory where it says in writing when you were home and met the girl? Everything's written up at a factory, and when you had time off would naturally be in their books."

That was true, and the landscape immediately around me brightened. Yes, I soon thought the old man was surrounded by a gold rim there where he sat with his white beard. We started figuring and came to the conclusion that it was ten months between my meeting with the girl and the kid's arrival.

"Then you'll make it," said the old man. "No bitch goes so long, let alone a first timer. Now go to the factory and get down on paper when you were off and went home. Right?"

"Yes, that has to work. You were smart to come up with that. Now they can come with their letters."

I saw a way to go on living. I would be acquitted and my girl friend would never have to know anything. Not my parents either. I was boundlessly glad to live that day, and I thought about what I could do for the old man in return. But an occasion didn't arise before winter, and there was not much I could do then.

I happened to go to the old man's place one day in the winter, and I saw immediately that something was wrong.

"Good that you came," said the old man, continuing to shake a bottle of medicine. "My old lady will leave me soon. Two nights I've sat up and tended her and now I'm real tired. I'm starting to get old too. Look, my hands are shaking."

I went into the bedroom and looked at the old woman. She was like a yellow skeleton, breathing only now and then. I knew it was just a matter of hours for her, but I wanted to pretend I was learned, so I took her shriveled wrist to feel her pulse. I couldn't find it.

"Of course she'll get better again," I said to the old man when I came out into the kitchen.

"Don't talk shit. But it would be nice of you to sit with her a few hours tonight so I could get a little sleep."

I walked out there that evening and I had a bottle of juice for the dying woman from Mother, who was always upset when someone was going to die. When she got to that point herself some years later, she was calmer than anyone else I had seen when they went through the door at the far end of the corridor.

The old man found an *Aller's Family Journal* yearbook for 1891 for me to look at. Then he mixed up some juice, which I was supposed to give the old woman in teaspoons, and took off his coat and boots.

"I won't undress just in case something happens," he said. "Wake me up when she gets worse."

He lay down on the quilt beside the old woman and was asleep in half a minute.

I slowly turned the pages in the old book, which smelled damp and musky. The ship's clock ticked and cracked sometimes in an old cabinet. The old man wheezed and slept, and the old woman occasionally drew in a long, trembling breath. Outside, the landscape lay chalk-white and frozen in the cold and moonlight. I wished the old pair had had a cat that could keep me company. I had suggested to the old woman once that they should get themselves one, but she, being very economical, answered peevishly: "A cat? No, of course not. Have such a thing scamper about your skirts after something to eat?"

Gradually the old woman began to wean herself of eating, but she nursed the old man and stuffed food into him. She might have lived a few years more if she had eaten more, I thought, looking at the sighing skeleton on the bed. The old man had hung a rag over the lamp so the light wouldn't shine so sharply in her eyes.

At the times the old man had told me, I poured the juice with a teaspoon into the shriveled hole that had uttered a few million tender and angry sounds during more than eighty years. I had looked through the journal and everything started becoming uncanny. As the iron stove cooled off in the kitchen, the cabin got cold. I looked out at the frost-still landscape and shone a light on the thermometer outside the window. Twenty-eight degrees.

Then suddenly from the bedroom came, "Aah . . . aah."

I shivered from head to toe, the sound was so unlike anything I had ever heard before. It embraced a mass of alien things, as if a human being had seen unbelievable and impossible things there was no word to describe. I plucked up my courage, however, and went into the bedroom. The old woman lay as before, but the old man had turned on his other side. His beard moved when he breathed.

I sat down again and tried to ignore the sound. The old woman had wailed, and what's more, she certainly had a right to; she was, after all, dying. The hair on my hands stood straight up; that made me think about our ancestors who were hairy all over their bodies. Ha, ha! They must have looked like something terrible when they got their backs up in fear or anger.

It was hard to get calm again. Those two old people looked so strange under those old quilts and in the half-dark illumination. Their faces were almost black. Under the sideboard a rat nibbled, and once I caught a glimpse of her as she ran quickly around a corner.

The ship's clock ticked all the harder, sometimes with a kind of double stroke as if picking up speed. Before it struck, it started to hiss and crackle heftily. The old man snored and moved his big veined hands fitfully. His watch and snuff box lay on a chair by the bed.

Then I heard a noise outside the cabin. It started just by the corner where I was sitting. A shuffling sound against the wall outside. I sat completely still and heard someone walking around outside the cabin, dragging something along the wall—a broom or spruce branch. I felt my legs shake and looked out the window. The night lay hard and white. The shuffling sound came again from the other side and stopped where it had begun.

"Aah . . . aaah," the old woman said suddenly without moving her lips. But now the terror was almost gone from her voice, and it sounded as if she had seen someone she felt measureless amazement and admiration for. The shudders in me came and went. As fast as one went out my leg, another started in my head again.

The ship's clock hissed and struck twelve-thirty.

"Aah," the old woman said, and now she was just triumphant.

I clenched my fists, got up from my chair, and went over to the bed without daring to look out the window when I walked past it. I took the old man by the arm, and he instantly lifted his head and looked at the old woman.

"I don't think she has long," I said and the old man nodded. He tried to pour juice in her, but she didn't swallow any longer and it ran out the corners of her mouth. Ten minutes later she was dead.

Now I started to bounce about, fussing again, wanting to show that I wasn't one to get shaken up when someone was dead. I found a scarf and tied it under the woman's chin so she wouldn't lie with her mouth open. Then I stretched her arms out to the side. The old man looked on and sighed.

"Now I'm all alone," he said. "She's been able and good. I don't have anything to complain about. It was fifty-three years we were together. It was good you woke me so I didn't sleep when she got to the end."

"It's better anyway when the old women die first," I said. "A man always gets by better than a woman can."

"You're right about that," the old man answered, brightening.

"Besides there are always old women around if you want to have one. Now I'll make a fire in the stove and we'll have ourselves a drop of coffee. What time was it when she died?"

I took down the old man's silver watch, which hung above the bed, but it had stopped. The spring had broken when the old woman died.

"It's twenty years since I put a spring in last," said the old man. "Now it's broken. Yes, a clock usually does stop when someone dies."

Yes, my being there probably made the night a little easier for the old man, and I never told him what I had heard before the old woman died. Afterwards I thought a lot about it and finally was content that mystical forces come to life when a person dies. That proved something, I thought.

That old woman saw something far beyond what she had seen or imagined up until then—that I could be sure of. Don't go saying anything else. Her tongue wanted to describe it but it was too late. It just came out "aah," but before or since I've never heard or read any thesis that said more than that.

This happened, as I said, later in the winter and was the only thing I could do for the old man. Of course, I walked along behind his poor man's coffin, too, but I got a little coffee in the poor old hut for that, so it's nothing to open my mouth about.

The night before I left, I met the girl and lied as if I were standing before God's judgment seat. I was going to do this and this in town, didn't she understand, ha ha.

It may be the last night I'll have her, I thought, and I nearly wore her out with my hard hands. Silly promises were made on both sides, promises you'd have to be a god or a devil to keep. I saw the August moon make her face pale, and I probably looked unusually good, too, judging from her devotion.

We had found a nice alcove among a few small spruce trees where we always tacitly agreed to go. During the days I went there alone, looking for traces from her body. This night we were still sitting when the sun came up, and we came close to being discovered. An old crofter woman came pattering on naked, gray feet, and when there was only a spruce bush between her and us, she stopped, cupped her hands to her mouth, and screamed resoundingly, "Kokossan . . . coooome!"

So she listened for a reply while we breathlessly and anxiously stared at her through the needles. If she had looked our way, she would have first seen a little blue garment which was slung to the side and on which a pair of morning flies sat and occasionally hunted each other up with a cheery hum. Then she certainly would have looked for more.

But God came to our aid. The old woman pattered on and soon we heard her persuasive call resound farther away.

I came a half hour early to the meeting with the child welfare woman, and I walked back and forth a few times looking at myself in the store windows. Then I saw the woman Hilma Andersson coming, and I knew I was in for a confrontation. She saw me too and her loose mouth was drawn into a scornful smile. She was gaudily and flimsily dressed according to the latest fashion, but her body was still limp from childbirth.

In due time, I was shown by sharp eyes and disdainful gestures behind desks and counters into a room where a middle-aged woman reigned. She moved her head a bit when I greeted her and set a pair of clear, cold eyes on me.

"You are factory worker Lars Johan Hård?"

"Yes."

The woman gestured towards Hilma Andersson, who sat in a chair.

"Miss Andersson singles you out as being the father of her child, born August 4. Do you admit fatherhood?"

"No, it can't be me. It's absolutely impossible."

"Did you meet her at that time?"

"Meet her, of course, but not so a kid could come of it. But I know five other men she's had and who fit the time right . . . ."

"I haven't asked about that. Did you have such a relationship with her that a child could have resulted?"

"No, there couldn't be anything from it. It doesn't fit the time right either. I have it down on paper here when it was; I was off only once the whole autumn."

The girl, who had sat with a cocksure grin on her face, moved a little anxiously in her chair. The child welfare woman took the statement and figured something out on the paper. She figured out on paper whether I was the kid's father.

Then she turned to Hilma Andersson.

"You insist that this man is the father of your child?" she asked, and her voice was very gentle.

"Oh, yes. Because right after it, my monthlies didn't come . . . ."

"That's fine."

I, the male, felt the hostility and advantage both those females had; they stuck together against me, the bourgeois woman and the slut. With my voice quivering with emotion, I said to the latter, "You don't have the slightest bit of shame. You had different men every night and you know it can't be me . . . ."

"Quiet!" the child welfare woman screamed sharply. "What's the matter here? 'Do you acknowledge your fatherhood,' I asked, and will you come to terms with me about monthly support for bringing up the child?"

"When it's not mine? Like hell I will!"

"I should advise you to behave more civilly," said the bourgeois woman, showing great calm contempt. "If this certificate is authentic, it still doesn't mean anything. According to this, there are 299 days between your meeting with Miss Andersson and the child's birth, and in the law, 300 days is the limit."

"But we all know it's ten months and no woman goes so long. She'd have to be a mare to do that. What kind of damned laws are those?"

"I'm asking for the last time: will you amicably come to terms with me about a monthly allowance for bringing up the child?"

"No. You know perfectly well it's not mine."

"I don't know any such thing. You can go. Miss Andersson will stay while I set up the summons proceedings."

The girl grinned triumphantly. Her hands were on her lap and they were red with black-bordered nails even though she was a dishwasher. I had gotten very fine hands myself since being out of work. Hilma sat in an easy chair and I, the nasty seducer, on an ordinary one.

"May I ask something?" I asked, turning around in the door.

"What, then?"

"Well, if the court acquits me, then will you summons those five other men? If she over there admits she's had them?"

"Under such circumstances I will summons one of them," the bourgeois woman answered coolly. "Incidentally, this is no information bureau."

The Andersson girl giggled ingratiatingly, revealing that several of her teeth had blackened. I traveled home with my heart full of great despair and cursing. Everything I thought of saying in my defense was gone; I had been singled out as the father of the screeching product of the combination of Hilma Andersson and several men's internal secretions coming together, and neither God nor the devil could save me.

Should I let my girl friend know anything? That was the biggest and hardest question of all. Those days, I longed for purity as never before. Admit everything and see the disgust in her blue eyes? Never! To hell with all summonses from old women and Jesus. Refuse flat out. No one carries a child for ten months. That was the thought that lifted me and held me up those days. It helped me to talk, put on a show, eat, and be damned nasty—in a word, to live those days.

But what would I say when the county deputy came one day with his striped cap on to serve the writ on me? All the cabin windows would be full of curious popeyes; the girl and my parents would know everything. Besides, the deputy was an ass, and he would run around chattering pompously.

And so it happened that I wrote the child welfare woman a letter which was mild and angry at the same time. Was there any way to get out of the writ? God knew I wasn't guilty. Ten months—

she should certainly think something about that herself. She was a woman herself, even though the law had gone to hell, made up by eighteenth-century scoundrels. Yours respectfully. Return postage enclosed.

I got an answer quickly, a gray, commanding envelope. Inside were a letter and a form. The letter said that if I didn't want to admit that I *was* the father of the child Nils Josef Valdemar, she had enclosed a form saying I conceded that I *could* be the papa. Maybe I would feel better about signing that. If I sent it back signed and paid twenty-five crowns per month for sixteen years, I could avoid the writ. But at once. Ex officio.

I brooded, swore, cried, and wandered miles and miles in the middle of the nights. The girl's eyes were bluer and more devoted than ever when I met her, and I would rather have drowned myself like a rat than see them despise me. After losing five kilos, I sent the child welfare woman the form with my name under it. The devil standing behind my chair witnessed my signature.

In the forest, I didn't earn more money than what went for food and clothes, and consequently the child Nils Josef Valdemar Andersson went without any. I trembled before those gray, importunate letters which came every week. And how I hated them! They got sharper and threatened me with measures the situation demanded. My anxiety cut deeper furrows in my insides, and I soon began to notice things in my body I had never noticed before. The permanent blockage in my chest got all the heavier; my heart started to beat unevenly, and I thought I would fall down and die some sunny day. But I didn't tell anyone about that but lied instead when my heart gave a jump and started beating against my ribs.

"Why do you get red spots on your face and breathe hard like that?" Mother would ask.

"Ah, leave me alone."

"You know I see it. It would be better if you told me if you have a pain somewhere."

Later, when the letters started talking about the workhouse, I thought about my heart problem with joy, hoping it would save me.

I brooded sometimes about the paper I had signed. Why were two different papers printed up, one where it said that you *were* the father and one that you *could be* the father of a kid? Surely you either were or you weren't. Of course later, I came to know that both those papers had equal validity under the law. Then it's certainly a dirty trick to let a man sign the paper with the milder tone. Why was there such a thing, for that matter? I wrote to the child welfare woman and asked about it, and she answered that I, in order to avoid being detained at the workhouse through the requested assistance of the Office of the Governor, should immediately send in the amount due as the allowance for my child Nils Josef Valdemar Andersson's upbringing.

I lay in the grass more than half the working hours every day, and I could no longer think about discoveries or improvements; instead my emotions were torn and quivering before society's blind, hard claw grip. When I went back and forth to the forest, I looked anxiously around me to make sure there was no one coming along the road who I'd have to meet. The coachman and his housekeeper upset me most with their wicked, scornful grins. It was getting towards autumn now; the days were clear and light, the lingonberries got red on one side, and the ants crept more tranquilly on the spruce twigs than before.

On the stable wall was a place where all posters were usually nailed up. There you could see when the Salvation Army would be coming to the chapel to hold a revival, when the workers' union meeting would be held in the county room, or when auction debts should be paid. Sometimes when a circus would set up its tent on a hillside and entice you with world attractions and giant, gala performances among the juniper shrubs.

I came from the forest and saw almost all the farm's inhabitants assembled in front of some paper on the stable wall. I immediately felt a strong uneasiness, almost a fear of walking past the crowd of people standing there. I heard a few laugh while others, a couple of older ones, said that it was damned nasty and unnecessary.

They made room for me and they all watched me—with lots of different looks in their eyes. On the wall sat the letter from Hilma Andersson that I had torn apart among the bushes one time, and the bits were skillfully pasted together on a piece of paper. Her large, simple-minded writing said that she was too big to go out at night and that it was too late to do anything about it. And damn you if you don't answer. You're sure to be cocky enough when the child welfare bureau gets a hold of you. As ever . . . .

Someone my own age tore the paper down, and I walked on with a red face, breathing hard. I had first intended to laugh and pretend that the whole thing was funny and meaningless, then get angry and swear, but I couldn't do anything but swallow and walk away. No one behind me laughed; they were good people, all of them, and they said good night to each other and went home without comment. But there were some twenty-five men there, and I knew what the subject of conversation would be in just that many cabins that night.

Because I too was a kind of man, I had to be brash and do something in my own defense. When two aspirin powders had worked, I knocked on the coachman's door and looked as angry as I could.

"Do you know what that can cost you?" I asked.

But the coachman and his woman didn't get scared but continued eating and smacking their lips instead.

"That's defamation of character and I can sue you for it," I continued. "Besides, I've never done anything to you two."

"You've been cocky," the housekeeper answered flatly, licking her fat fingers. "You think you're above others because well-bred girls fuss over you. But I've seen bigger ships than a shit-bucket capsize."

And she took on a severely prophetic look as if she were my fate—a large, greasy, and wicked fate.

My courage, raised by aspirin, sunk before the two old people's inveterate malice, and I walked away from them. I heard them talking loudly and victoriously behind me—it didn't work for any saucy brats to come setting themselves against them no matter how big and tall. They'd been around too long for that.

"If he comes over here again," said the old coachman, munching, "I'll twist his nose for him."

I walked away from their door, thinking apathetically that then he would have to climb up on a chair and ask me to stand still.

That night the girl came and wanted to talk to me. Tears ran from her blue eyes, and I thought, "Now it's over." My breath stuck in my chest, but when the girl started talking, I grew calm again. She had gotten a letter ordering her to come home, and that was why her cheeks were wet. Because she must be separated from me.

We said good-by between seven and twelve at night, and we repeated all the promises from before and added some new ones. It was altogether unthinkable that we should forget each other. Such a sincerely loving couple had not existed since Romeo and Juliet. Now I only worried that the coachman would get to the farm with the gossip before the girl got on her way.

Little, delicate, and soft, she sat on my knee in our statare kitchen when Father and Mother had gone in and shut the bedroom door. She stroked my hair and said that you feel what we feel for each other only once in a lifetime. We didn't need to talk about fidelity; that went without saying between us.

I sat there and felt wretched and unclean inside. But I prayed in my soul that if I got to keep that little woman, thereafter I wouldn't pollute myself either outside or inside. In addition, I would ceaselessly strive to improve myself and become worthy of her. To begin with, I would go to the national archives the next time I went to town and try to find out if my grandfather, the Russian, was a count or a prince in his time after all. There was certainly something about me since well-bred girls came to me with no question.

Though I thought it unnecessary, the girl said she would tell about a fancy she had had earlier.

"There can't be the least shadow between us," she said and told a little banal story about a lieutenant. I already knew, of course, how limited her experience was; the young spruces and moss could testify to that.

When she was through, it was my turn, and I lied awfully, made myself out to be pure white while I was sniffling inside.

"But you had my friend," the girl said, mildly reproachful as she stroked my hair.

"No, dearest, already then I thought exclusively of you and couldn't touch anyone else."

"Just think, that's what she told me," said the girl pensively.

"Yes, a spurned woman, you see. She's capable of saying and doing anything at all to be revenged."

The flies buzzed near the iron stove, the cat slept in a ball on the wooden bench's red cover, and outside, the moths struck against the lighted window. The night was dark and warm when we came out and the crickets chirped in the grass. A dark sky had stopped above the cove and stared meditatively down into the obscurity of the water. In the west it was clear and some stars twinkled.

With a salty taste on my lips from the girl's parting tears, I went out on the field road in the still night. I stood unmoving for half an hour and stared up into the blue-gray gulf above me. When I had delved as deeply as I could into it, I said with premeditated calm, tears running out, I don't know why: "I won't play up to you any more, you supreme sadist up there. If you command me to walk to eternal damnation, I'll do it, and don't think I'll look back once. Do your worst; like I said, I'm not afraid of you."

So I said and didn't mind that the tears ran all the way down to my collar. I felt myself unshakable in a grand way; I expected the worst and was not afraid of anything less.

"Just go ahead—give it to me," I said several times on the way home, glancing furtively up at the dull-blue sky. But nothing happened and I noted scornfully, "You've tangled your legs in your own laws and now you have to follow along yourself. You don't do what you want to any more, not you either, ha ha . . . ."

A couple of days later when I came in at night Father was still sitting at the table though it was very late. He held his big, black-bearded head in his hands and sang protractedly and sorrowfully:

> *"Lord, let your white dove*
> *Rest in the end with You."*

"Where did you get the schnapps?" I asked.

"From town. You know that. Will you have a drink with your father?"

"I don't know. Haven't you had some friends in here then?"

"Yes, a couple of the old men were here but their old ladies came and got them. They would have caught hell for that if it had been me. No old lady messes with me. Yeah, go ahead and snort in there," he laughed towards the room where Mother lay.

> *"This world has no grassy knoll*
> *Where she can safely rest . . . ."*

". . . Bottoms up, boy. When I was your age—well, damn it."

Because I was sad and longed uncontrollably for the girl, I drank with my father. First he was happy and boastful, telling stories from his youth about fights where he had always come off the victor. Gradually he got melancholy.

"You're an old man now and a man can talk to you," he said. "It's good to talk to somebody sometimes. You've probably seen that it's been a little any which way between your mother and me sometimes. A man can't talk about such things with kids. But now you're big and beginning to understand a little. We'll just take another shot."

"Johan," Mother's voice said warningly from the bedroom, "don't sit digging up old shit."

"You be quiet in there and go to sleep. Yes, I should say that you've had a little to do with women yourself now," Father said, "and of course I've seen and understood more than you think. You won't go hitching yourself to any woman if you'll take my advice. It's like binding up your own tail."

"Yes, that's probably true."

"As the gospel. I for example wouldn't have had to be a statare my whole life if it weren't for women."

Here Father lowered his voice so he wouldn't be heard in the bedroom, then continued.

"Once when I was a young man I was invited to join a circus troupe. They were Germans. I was damn strong, you see. But then she, your mother, was already on the way with the first kid and so, of course, I got no place."

"But surely it wasn't all her fault."

"Don't you see. If she hadn't been on the way, I would have gone off with the circus. I never would have had to become a statare and rough it my whole life like I've had to do."

A sigh came from the bedroom and Mother said to me, "Don't let him make you think that everything is women's fault, Lars. He does nothing but complain about them and even so he's run after them his whole life."

"Run! I only study types of human beings," Father responded in defense. "I have always been interested in the study of human beings in connection with . . . ."

"Cow pens," Mother interjected from the bedroom, and I remembered a piece of gossip about my father and a milkmaid. Someone supposedly had seen them in a cow pen. Father had always brushed aside the accusation with great anger, but now he looked at me, embarrassed, and said, "Quarrel with old ladies and piss in the wind, you'll get everything back on you. A man exists to drudge for the old ladies and kids; if he takes a drink sometimes, it's a turn towards hell . . . .

> . . . *but she longs, yes, she longs to be home*
> *Away from worry, violence, and storm* . . . ."

"Don't yell so you wake the neighbors," mother warned. "They sure don't need to know you're drunk. What gall to sing in the middle of the night, and religious songs besides."

But now Father was happy again. His brown eyes danced, and his teeth glistened in his beard.

74

"What shall I sing for you then, my little whiner?" he said to-wards the bedroom. "This here:

> *I got me a hat from Poland,*
> *Through it shines sun and moon,*
> *So we roll the small . . . ."*

"Shut up and lie down," Mother interrupted. "And you too, Lars, it's not good manners to sit drinking with your father."

" . . . *keg again,*" Father finished.

I went to the wooden bench and lay down but Father stayed where he was. He laid his heavy head down on the table top and sang quietly, yawned, swore, and laughed now and then at a thought running into his head.

The rumor ran through the cabins on quick, black feet, and soon I could see in the eyes of people I met that I was the father of Hilma Andersson's bastard. I witnessed from our bedroom window how the coachman's housekeeper on eager rhinoceros legs waddled away to the garden and animatedly told something to the brown-eyed girl and the slender girl. Inside I alternately raged and thanked God that the little one had gone and was out of reach.

A gardener working nearby heard the housekeeper's descrip-tion and told me later how differently the two girls had reacted. The slender one had made it clear immediately that she had loathed me from the start with my half-cultivated and stilted man-ner. Someone had dared talk, connecting her name with mine. At this farm, people talked terribly and lied appallingly. She for one had never been around anyone worse.

The brown-eyed one had said nothing, and when her friend ap-pealed to her, asking if it wasn't shocking, she shrugged her shoul-ders and turned away. I was sympathetically disposed to her at once, and when I met her one Sunday afternoon in the September sun, I greeted her very courteously. She stopped and said that the weather was glorious, and then we occupied ourselves a while with meteorological observations. Her voice had a warm, interested ring that I hadn't heard before, and she stood very close to me. Inside I wondered with surprise if she hadn't understood the latest news in all its ghastliness.

"I thought of walking a bit," she said. "Will you walk with me?"

Her smile was beautiful, the day was mild, and my chest warmed up inside. I took her firm hand in mine, and we walked like a pair of children across the field. She stumbled occasionally and then took a better hold of my hand. The warmth from her went through my arm and out in my body and made me remember how long it had been since the little one had gone away.

"The lady has gone to church," said the girl when we came into the forest. "That's why I dared go out. She watches us day and night since . . . ."

She checked herself and I saw from the side that her cheek turned a deeper color. Oh—I knew what she was thinking, all right. Since it had come out that I was the papa of Hilma Andersson's brat, she meant. The bitterness, which was never too far away, promptly marched into my soul.

"Oh, yes, she has gone to church, the lady of the house," I said. "What for, then, really? I sat near her in church one time and she couldn't sing a note. She howled along with the psalm anyway just like a hound. You know, I think better of a wild man on Easter Island who comes timidly out of the forest and throws himself on his face in front of a rock carving or crooked tree than those modern ladies who torment their underlings all week long and on Sunday go to church and buy forgiveness for the last week's meanness with protracted howls to an imaginary God."

"Are you off again now?" the girl said smiling.

"No. But think yourself what a comedy it is. Some dull, half-dead old men and old ladies from the poorhouse sit farthest back in the big cool stone house where no god can feel at home. Farthest forward are benches for the upper-class people who in the same church forget that the last shall be first. All of them are united, however, in making a fuss about that God because He's going to give them a place in His heaven sometime. They'll sit in the same order there, of course, the poor ones farthest down. Oh, yes, meanwhile, the minister stands in the vestry, full and satisfied, picking his teeth after breakfast. So he hangs his finery on, makes some distorted expressions with his mug, walks up to the altar, and screams holy . . . holy . . . holy . . . ha ha ha! Then he still has the stomach to talk about the heathens."

The girl said nothing, but a smile lay behind her expression. She's gotten to be so nice, I thought. Then I thought out loud. "I want to be that wild man."

"That's what you are, too," the girl answered. "You're a real wild man. I get almost frightened of you."

I liked that. My bitterness laid itself to rest again, and I thought about what I should do to further strengthen the impression of wildness I had made on the girl. I had a vague notion that I should either climb up in a tree or raise a yell. I managed, however, to refrain from doing either.

We stood beside a large rock and it led my thoughts back a few eras. Most likely my father had read *The Wonder of the Universe* the night before he and my mother got ready to have me, since my thoughts slipped so eagerly onto quasi-geological paths.

I gave a long speech, and the girl looked at me with a friendly smile the whole time. I finished by laying my hand on the rock and pontificating, "In this rock's heart lie fossils, petrified creatures who millions of years ago saw the same sun that now shines on us."

"No," the girl said quietly, "there can't be fossils in this rock. It's granite, primary rock, that the ice broke loose, and no trace of life has ever been found in it. It's just in volcanic kinds of rock that petrified organisms can be found."

It was a regular cold shower. She could not have touched me in a more tender spot, and I felt how the blood rushed up into my head. It seemed to me she had yanked the soul right out of my body and hit me in the mouth with it for my big talk. Was there then not one single area where I could be superior?

But the girl was magnanimous and did not follow through on

her victory. Instead she moved a little closer to me and asked, "Can't we talk about something else that's more fun than pre-historic periods and rocks?"

I thought I heard a hidden meaning in her voice, and I wondered what she was getting at. She stood right next to me, her chest bulged under her blouse, and her brown gaze was like velvet. I stroked her hair and she didn't give me a punch in the nose; she didn't even wrinkle her black streak of an eyebrow. Instead she put out her hand and stroked me on the cheek. A strong need to complain came over me; I felt endlessly sorry for myself and I turned away with moist eyes.

"What is it?" she asked, touching my arm.

"I have it so da . . . so hard," I explained with a quivering voice after I swallowed a moment. "Everything is against me."

"Yes, yes, I know, I've heard. But don't be sad, little one. We'll sit down here. Now tell me everything."

And she broke down the ferns below the rock for us to sit on.

I sat down a half meter from her; since she had taken me down a peg with her geological knowledge, I had a certain respect for her. With roused voice, I shared with her the repulsiveness of my life during the last year. Above all I emphasized that I had never touched Hilma Andersson, but that explanation didn't make much of an impression on the girl. She seemed to prefer thinking me guilty. She returned incessantly to the principal point in the matter, the meeting with Hilma Andersson.

"So very little is necessary for . . . for . . . ," she said.

"Yes, that's true all right, but remember that it was ten months anyway."

"Maybe you counted wrong."

Now I got quiet and sullen, but the girl lay down on the ferns, took a blade of grass and tickled me on the nose.

"Don't be sad, little one," she said. "It's no use taking anything seriously here in this world. You only live once and so you ought to make the most of every minute instead."

She wasn't haughty as usual but instead even laughed a couple of times. Even though she knew my predicament.

Besides that, I sure could guess what she meant, "You only live once." So says a woman when she wants to kick out all thoughts of the time to come and take hold of an opportunity that may not come again. I started to follow my intuition and I was right. The brown-eyed, haughty, upper-class girl meanwhile breathed calmly, and the movements she made were certainly poised, skilled, and sufficiently obliging.

Then the church bell began ringing. First the little bell tolled a couple of times, and then the big bell joined in. The old, rigid, and vengeful doomsday God, who had gotten into my blood, spoke rumblingly in my Luther-pressed soul, and my hands went still among the girl's silks.

"In the middle of the church service, I break one of the strict commandments and commit a mortal sin," I thought, feeling heaven open accusingly above my back.

The September sun was mild and good, the bells resounded, everything was fresh and pure. The spruces stood mute and eternal above us, the sky was full of high eternity, and the sexual act which was just now so desirable turned thin and untempting in the new atmosphere. The girl probably felt the sensation even more strongly than I did, since she gave me a poke in the chest, got up, and sputtered, "What are you doing? Do you think you're dealing with some servant girl?"

I was surprised and angry. Hadn't I, after all, drawn back of my own free will?

"Yes, why shouldn't I think that?" I asked back. "What would be the big difference?"

"I felt real pity for you," the girl said in a tone between complaint and contempt. "But you obviously don't deserve it. I'm disappointed in you."

"I know you must be," I answered. "But honest, it was the church bells' fault. If they hadn't started ringing so inconveniently . . . ."

Fire-red with rage, the girl walked away from me and half a fern branch hung green and glaring from the back of her wine-red coat. I saw her disappear beyond the trees and thought about all three times we had met and separated as bitter enemies.

I wandered about aimlessly in the forest until the sun was a good way down. On the way home, I stopped in a grove with reddish-yellow deciduous trees that hid a gray barn among them. The dying blades of grass glistened in the sun, the dragonflies flew back and forth silently, the rose hip and barberry shone.

In the forest on the other side of the ditch a cow bellowed. The bellowing was full of autumn's melancholy, past ages' desolation, vaguely outlined longing, and something still more than words can describe. The transparent autumn day that drew to its close, the heavy blue skies, the red rose hips among the frostbitten leaves, the gray barn, and spider web strands in the grass—everything floated together with the distant animal cry and created a massive weight somewhere behind, before, and above me. My frailty grew frightened before all that lay behind the visible. I took a rose hip and looked at it. Rose hip, I thought, yes, there's one side to it, I can see that. But the other side. Rose hip, what good will it do me to dismiss you with a name?

The clear landscape terrified me all the more, the blood rose to my head, and I started whistling and running to save myself.

A few days later, I heard that the brown-eyed girl had gone. I regretted then that I hadn't tried to bring out her better side with gentleness and friendship. But when I heard she had called me a boor and a farm hand, I knew that I had instinctively behaved just right towards her and decided to strike her from memory.

Late at night the light went on at the coachman's, the door of the carriage shed stood open, and I realized the coachman was taking someone to the last train. The housekeeper always sat up when the coachman was gone; she couldn't fall asleep for fear of the tramps and hawkers who walked the roads. If she had one inside as a night guest, on the other hand, it was always quiet and the lights were off even if the coachman was out chauffeuring at night.

I walked through the porch as quietly as I could and sat down to think by our kitchen table. Watery porridge was left in a dish from the evening meal. Mother had probably thought I would want some food when I came in. In a pitcher the skim milk shone blue, and a pair of autumn flies, which the lamplight had awakened, risked their lives on the slick porcelain to stick their suckers into the liquid. I helped up the one who fell in and it sat down to dry its wings off in my hand. I thought that I must be a nice, good human being who had a heart even for the smallest things.

I heard the coachman drive up the hill with his old coach, and he cracked the whip a few times from old habit. My thoughts started directing themselves to all the pain he and his fat woman had caused me, and soon I felt a strong urge to be revenged in some way. Should I sneak out and scare the horses for him so they would dash off? No, that was almost too much. I hit on something less dangerous.

My eye fell on the dish with the gray-brown porridge before me, and I got an idea. I laughed silently a long time before I put it to work.

I took a fistful of the messy porridge and then noiselessly opened the door. The stream of light fell on the coachman's door directly across the porch and I sneaked forward over the rag rug, and, silently grinning, carefully smeared the coachman's whole doorknob with the porridge. The housekeeper yawned with a long-drawn-out screech, and the smell of coffee came from inside. I came happily in again after my sticky expedition and sat down at the table to listen. I put out the lamp and awaited the coachman's arrival with the flies buzzing back and forth in the darkness.

I didn't sit there without thinking the trick was childish and unworthy of a mature person. But it was too late to do anything; the coachman's step could be heard on the hill, and he spit out his snuff by the steps before he came in.

I listened excitedly. Now he was on the porch; now he gripped the door handle. I heard a surprised "Usch" and he must have been taken by a horrible misperception.

"Damn, if that's shit—" he yelled aloud and threateningly.

The housekeeper came out and they started a heated dialogue with me as the main subject. They could not understand how

81

someone like me was allowed to go loose. They recommended Svartsjö[1] as an appropriate place for me, and if there was any justice left I would go there. Such an outrage should be in the newspaper. There weren't any more vile people than those who would not let old honorable people live in peace.

Hold on, you old swine, I thought in the darkness. Why should the young respect you so much when you, at every opportunity, gorge yourselves on our youthful follies like a vulture on liver? With senile malice, you pry into our lives and censure us more stringently than Luther's *Long Catechism* ever did. Of course, you wore long skirts and went to church when you were young, but the little bodily part you so anxiously hid must have reacted then just as it does now.

The coachman gradually calmed himself and went in. They said before they closed the door that the porridge would stay there until the next day so it would be clear to people what a good-for-nothing they had for a neighbor.

I won't ask the honorable reader to follow me twenty years back in time. I'll be glad instead if the eventual reader will, in my questionable company, walk about one year forward in time. It was summer again, but a summer without work, without upper-class girls and romance. My two suits were threadbare in the seat and the watch made of imitation gold had stopped.

The whole year I had worked on my personal improvement and refinement, but no one except me seemed to notice the result. People said that I was a ne'er-do-well, woman chaser, and parasite. They said it so many times that my parents thought it was true and began regarding me with disapproving looks no matter what I did.

Then I got two letters at the same time. The one was from the

1. Svartsjö is a workhouse on a large island in Lake Mälar. It was originally a castle, built in 1734–39, but it has been used as a workhouse since 1891 and as an alcoholics' colony since 1920.

tiny girl and the other from society in its capacity as protector of the small. The girl wrote that I must come to her; it was a long way, to be sure, but it was absolutely necessary that she talk to me. I should advise her on an important matter; I was so understanding, so good. Soon, I should come soon. Always your girl.

The other letter was not much better. "Herewith you are advised that, unless you discharge within fourteen days your duty towards your child, Nils Josef Valdemar Andersson, after the expiration of the designated time, you will immediately, through the power of the appropriate governmental agency, be sent to a workhouse in order there to perform the work which will be assigned to you . . . ."

When I came out of the turmoil the letters had sent me into, I started cherishing my heart problem as the only thing that could save me from the inexorable that approached me. Forced labor is rough, I thought, and no one with a heart problem can manage it. Then maybe they'll let me go free. And I was happy every time my heart jumped and started beating unevenly.

That the girl wanted to meet me also girded me up a little. I would in some way get the travel money and go to her. She would give me strength and courage to meet whatever should come. I had her at least, even if I should lose everything later.

After many quotations from *The Wonder of the Universe*, my father gave me money for the trip.

"You walk around like a wounded moose," he said. "If it's the girl you're longing after so, go, but don't get your hopes up. You'll never get anything from her. It was the scarcity of men out in the sticks that made her get together with you, and nothing else. They have to have men whether they're high-class or low-class."

I didn't get angry with Father for his words; he meant well and, of course, he could not know how wonderful she was, the little one.

A hot July day saw me wash the best of the two suits with gasoline, and the morning after I went to the train. Mother raised a fuss about the cost, but Father pointed out behind his newspaper that it wouldn't mean a thing in fifty years. What do we mean? No more than fly shit.

When I walked away from home, I thought I was looking pretty good, but on the train I saw that my old suit didn't have much to recommend it in comparison with most of my fellow passengers' summer-gray elegance.

Between fragrant haycocks the train flew forward through small towns and past blue lakes. I tried to be happy that I was on my way to her who was everything to me, but a dull anxiety lurked in the hot day. Small irritations made their contributions too. The spots, which were completely gone the day before, shone scornfully now in the blazing hot sunshine, my hands got big and red, and the veins lay on them like ropes. Soot flakes from the locomotive settled on my sleeves and collar, and when I sat down on a bench a button on my trousers popped. I tried to make myself think that everything presaged luck for the journey. Besides, it would be late evening before I arrived, and then the darkness would mercifully erase my external inadequacies.

The sun was in the treetops when the train stopped by a little shady station. No one else got off but me, and on the platform stood only the gray stationmaster. Well, I surely couldn't expect the girl to walk three miles to the station. Naturally, she had carefully described the way.

I walked and walked; I got more and more dispirited in the strange surroundings. It was a big, fine house that the girl lived in; I had seen it in a picture. How could I, a cottage boy, make myself gentlemanly enough so the girl wouldn't have to be ashamed of me? Counts and barons were frequent visitors there, I had heard. I scissored my long legs along more and more hesitantly on the strange country road.

I came into a forest that stood silent and solemn on both sides of the road. It was dusk now and nothing else but the thrush's clear song could be heard. Occasionally a forest mere's shiny black eye stared out at me from the forest. If I stopped, I could hear the voices of millions of mosquitoes singing a squeaking night hymn above and around me. The forest was stately and inaccessible here, not brushy and familiar like at home.

Suddenly a black bird came fluttering noiselessly and sat down right in front of my feet on the gray-white road. Startled, I stopped. Was it a sign that I should not go any farther? The black one sat silently, flicking its tail occasionally. When I set one foot forward, it fluttered a half meter away and sat down again.

I walked slowly forward and the bird fluttered and hopped before me. I stared at it constantly, and suddenly it flew into the forest with a twisting cry.

Nightjar, I thought, it was a nightjar. But why did it act so strangely?

Meanwhile I had forgotten to look down the road and hadn't seen a little figure coming towards me. When the nightjar flew away and I looked up, the small girl stood before me.

At least a hundred times during the trip I had practiced what I would say and do when I met her, but now I remembered nothing. I pulled off my hat and held it in my fist. It was old and I undoubtedly looked better without it.

"Than you for coming," the girl finally said, putting her hand out. But I didn't take it, mostly because my own hand was so hot and sweaty again. I also sensed a smell of poverty, cabin and gasoline rising up from my suit. The class difference grew up like a plank between us; she was fresh, clean, and schooled, I rough, sweaty, and disconsolate. I did not take her hand but lied in a voice that was rough after a day of silence: "Sooner or later I would have come here anyway. I've wanted to see this area for a long time."

"Yes, it's very beautiful here," the girl answered conversationally.

She was every inch upper-class now and I felt generations of lower-class clumsiness rise up within me. I thought bitterly that my grandfather was probably no eminent Russian—no, he was surely nothing more than a poor, suppressed, cringing Russian farmer.

"You wrote that I could advise you," I said. "What in? I can't advise anyone."

We had started walking along the edge of the road; I looked at the dusty plants in the ditch and tried to remember their Latin names. I thought about all possible trifles to get a respite from something I felt approaching me.

"Maybe we don't need to go home to your house," I continued. "We can just as well stand outside and talk. The weather's fine."

I thought I noticed the girl breathing easier after hearing me say that. The counts would surely have wrinkled their crooked noses at me. When I read philosophical books, I found that all human beings were the same refuse, but just now I could not deny the clothes', the nails', and the manners' superiority and meaning. I didn't have Father's easy readiness for putting an equals sign between people and flyspecks.

"If you want to, I'll gladly stay outside," said the girl.

We walked silently beside each other and when we came to a forest road off to one side, we walked in. When I saw a pool with clear water, I went up and washed my hands. Maybe I dimly hoped that the girl would lend me her handkerchief now, too, just like the time when I hopped over the fench for her. But she stood still on the road like a little white pillar in the darkness, and I dried most of the water off in the moss.

In a while we came to a flat rock with moss on it and then we sat down. The odor of flowers hung in the evening air, the kind that lodges itself in your chest and makes it heavy there. The girl picked in the moss and said nothing.

We couldn't have sat so close last summer without taking hold of each other, I thought, and it made my chest burn. But I stopped up the thought immediately and picked a soft live-forever in the moss.

It's a *sedum* I said to myself. *Sedum palustre.* It was used against unrequited love in the past. No one believes in such things any more.

"I thought of writing to you about everything," the girl said without looking at me, "but then I thought that it was cowardly to write about such things. That's why I asked you to come here."

My heart beat hard and anxiously as if it already knew something. I got very short of breath. As always when I sensed danger, a melody started playing inside me, banal and tormenting: "A street boy treads . . . treads into the hall . . . ."

The girl took out her handkerchief and held it to her eyes. She sobbed a couple of times, and once I put out my sweaty hand to caress her consolingly but pulled it back again.

"I won't torment you any longer," sobbed the girl. "I must be honest with you . . . I have had . . . I have been unfaithful to you."

I licked my lips and answered poorly, "Oh yes, uh-huh . . . 'a street boy treads' . . . you've had another then?"

The girl nodded in her handkerchief and went on sobbing a little more effectively.

"I don't understand it," I said, "I don't comprehend it."

"I don't comprehend it myself," she said with a steadier voice now that the worst was over. "I haven't cared for anyone the way I do for you, but I did it with someone else anyway . . . ."

"Yes, yes," I answered, extremely afraid to hear more. "It was here then that I should advise you?" I asked.

"Yes, you are so understanding, so broad-minded. What should we do now? You get to decide that."

Now I got angry, worker-angry and proud. Had she thought for a second that I would want to have her after she had been fooling around with someone else? She probably thought she was good enough for me even so, since she was upper-class. I got up and buttoned my coat.

"Is there a train going back tonight?" I asked.

"No," the girl answered quietly. "You mean you don't forgive me?"

"Forgive you, yes, by all means. It's only a word, of course, 'forgive,' and you can say it just as well as anything else if you have to flap your jaws."

"Don't be so bitter," the girl entreated. "You can't imagine what I've been through, no matter what the reason was . . . ."

What I felt in that strange forest was not clear to me. It was almost like when a close relative dies; you talk, eat and participate in the general hypocrisy of the burial without understanding what has happened. You can't make it out. But I thought of an honorable retreat in the midst of my misfortune.

"The cause," I said, "was surely the usual one. The cause surely came from its usual place, I can believe. Uh-huh, no more trains leaving this godforsaken place?"

"Not before nine o'clock tomorrow morning. In other words, you don't want to listen to me?"

"What should I listen to? Where you lay, what you said, and when it was? What does it matter to me?"

It grew quiet again; the girl had quit crying, but she kept picking in the moss. I looked from her breast to her hips and legs in the thin summer dress, thinking that other hands had glided hot over her, unbuttoned here, loosened a strap there and finally . . . .

"Well, I'll be on my way then," I said and stretched my hand out in parting.

The girl sobbed and stretched out both hands, but I took only the right one, pressing it a bit before I turned around and left. I straightened up and whistled to show how unaffected I was, but inside it felt like my life depended on the girl's calling me back. I listened tensely and slowed my steps but heard nothing. Finally I turned around, but then I saw only the forest in the dusk.

In a novel, the girl would have called my name wildly, I would have stopped, and everything would have ended happily and well. But this was merely poor reality and no one called. Instead I sneaked back after a while but didn't find the rock again. I found the forest and when I bent over, I saw her small footprints where a vein of water trickled, making the road a little muddy. She had gone home.

I followed after her with giant steps until I saw her in front of me. Then I slowed down again and in my heart I prayed heaven to send a tramp along to assault her so I would have a chance to rush up and save her. But the night sky took no notice of my little affair, the forest stood mute, the girl did not turn around and did not stop. I shadowed her and saw her stop by the gate of a big white house. I took position behind a birch bush and saw a man, or maybe it was a count, come out of the garden as if he had been waiting for the girl.

"Have you sent him away?" the man asked, taking her hand. I didn't hear the girl's answer, but the man responded, "Yes, but surely he couldn't be anything for you anyway. An uneducated worker."

After making this point, the man drew the girl with him towards the house. Now a battle rose up between the animal male inside me and the cultural coat outside. The male screamed loudly that I should rush out and strangle the other man with my bare hands, and my fingers cracked when I clenched them together. The newspapers would write about a deed perpetrated with bestial brutality, since I was an insignificant and unknown man. But if the count, or whatever he was, had killed me—then they would talk about a regrettable incident which took place during a sudden loss of mental control.

But nothing happened; the protecting melody started up in my head and I formed my jaw for whistling. In other words, I stood behind the birch bush whistling "Kväsarvalsen"[1] while the other one drew the girl with him to her bed, and I distinctly felt the red blood trickling in my chest.

I walked up on a ridge which slept with some spruce and birch trees on its back. Masses of mosquitoes, flying from the leafy bushes when I brushed against them, circled with a whining sound around me. I sat down on the ridge's highest point and looked out over the unfamiliar countryside. Far away a lake glistened, colored dark-red by the sky where the sun would come up.

Now I could no longer escape; all the repulsion rushed against me in the still night. The girl had taken up with someone else and was lost for all time; the county sheriff at home would soon take me to Svartsjö; I did not own anything. There was nothing on the plus side of my life, but even so I didn't want to die the death. I started to inflict plain, livid torment on myself by imagining the girl in all possible situations with the other man.

But he was too late for the flower of innocence, I thought with gloomy triumph. The statare boy had already played around with

---

1. "Kväsarvalsen" is the melody that keeps repeating itself in Lars's head. It was a popular tune, written by A. Högstedt and published in 1899.

that. But Father certainly was right when he said that had depended on my being on hand just when it was ready.

A light came on and I tried to guess which window the girl lay behind with her new lover. My chest was like a big wound, yet I tormented myself constantly with sensual pleasure. Jealousy, I said to myself, what is there really to it? The philosopher explained it this way, the one who didn't dare publish his writings while he was still living:[1]

The black sickness, or jealousy, is the name of the feeling of discomfort a man feels at the thought of or with the knowledge that another man, through bodily contact with the woman he has chosen as his own, deposits his bodily secretions in her or makes it one with hers.

So spoke the wise man, but there really isn't enough romance in that analysis, so no one needs to read it. I gorged myself further, however, on my suffering and imagined every movement of those two bodies down in the house. I remembered the girl's way of closing her eyes and turning her head to the side at a certain moment, and how then, still with closed eyes, she would stroke my head. She most likely still had the same habit. Ha, ha, if I should meet the man, so help me I'd ask him about it.

I took out my pocket mirror and looked at myself in it, and when I saw my red-bordered eyes, I got furious. "Are you crying, you tall, sentimental devil?" I said out loud up by the ridge. "Why, may I ask? Have you lost a girl? Remember that the little body there you're sniffling over will get old and dry and then die and rot. What do you want with that? You damned well can't lose anything here in this world because you don't have anything."

I got up and walked down the ridge again. I didn't let myself feel anything but instead walked quickly towards the station. When I walked past the white house, I stuck my tongue out at it. It said "Beware of Dog" on the gate and I thought that it should more appropriately read "Beware of Woman." Inside, the garden flowers glistened on both sides of the raked paths. The whole countryside slept; I alone wandered about with pain in my heart.

1. Peter Graves points out in *Jan Fridegård: Lars Hård* (Hull, 1977, p. 43) that the philosopher is Benedict Spinoza. The quotation is a radical paraphrase of Spinoza's *Ethics*, 3.35.

When I came to the forest road, I walked in on it again. I found both sets of footprints and the rock we had sat on; I saw the impression her body had made in the moss and then my heart smarted again so that I moaned. I immediately looked around distrustfully but no one was within hearing. Down by the rock, blueberry bushes grew, and I mechanically ate some blueberries. The sun came up and it looked as though the day would be just as warm as the last one.

A little farther on a crofter's holding lay in a forest opening and I walked towards it. Haycocks stood in rows on the little field, and on the cottage steps a white cat lay in the sun. I sat on a haycock a while and heard countless tiny sounds all around me. All nature was glad and fawning; I alone sat like an aching tumor in the midst of it. I took a handful of fragrant hay from the field and then the thought struck me that the girl had probably given herself to the other man in the hay. They had been out on a walk and had rested in a haycock or in a remote hay barn. There she had gone weak from the fragrance of hay and the summer night, pantingly weak and heavy-bodied.

Those thoughts drove me up out of the haycock and I walked towards the little cabin. Two beehives stood by the gable and the bees were already at work. A few meters from the cottage steps were a well with a windlass and a bucket for fetching water. I cranked up a bucketful, the cat following all my movements with suspicious eyes. I drank up the cold water and then dampened my handkerchief in the bucket to cool off my face. Then a window in the crofter's hut creaked open and a thin woman's face could be dimly seen next to a large bouquet of lady's bedstraw and oxeye daisies standing in a pitcher.

"What are you doing there?" the old woman croaked threateningly. "Be on your way now and don't prowl around the corners."

"Excuse me, but I'm only drinking a little water," I answered. "I'm a stranger to this area."

But the old woman was malevolent among her flowers.

"Just get away from the well or my man will come out with his gun," she vowed, opening the window a little more so her thin arm could be seen up to the elbow.

I walked back to the rock again and ate up all the blueberries around it. Then I lay down on the rock and hoped that I would fall asleep and get away from myself for a while, but the mosquitoes and forest ants took turns tormenting me. Soon the sun went behind a denser clumb of trees, moving the rock into the cold shadow.

Twice more I walked that dusty, sunny road back to the white house and saw the girl's small footprints in several places. The second time, the dog barked at me and tugged at the chain that bound him to the doghouse. I cursed him for making a racket and hid behind the birch again. There I stood, wondering what could be left for me. Society threatened me with forced labor, women were unfaithful to me, and dogs barked at me. The cat on the stone steps glared angrily at me, the mosquitoes and ants attacked me. At home my parents started looking on in morose silence whenever I ate because I could never pay for the food. Soon I wouldn't be able to dress well and my watch was broken. All I had was sixty-two öre and the return ticket in my wallet.

When the dog got tired of barking and then slinked into his house, I walked back on the road, vowing to go to the station and stay there those endless hours until the train left. Why did I run out here? Even if the girl came out again, it wouldn't change anything. She was contaminated now; my clear spring was, so to speak, muddied, most likely by a superficial man, spiritually inferior to me.

When I had walked a bit I heard a window open and, turning around, I saw a moustached man standing in his shirt looking at me. He probably thought I was a farm hand, walking back in the early morning from seeing my girl, since he looked at me so calmly, scratching his chest.

Then I fantasized that the girl would come to the train before it left. She had said herself it would leave at nine o'clock; maybe she had meant something by that. It had to be around five o'clock now, the sun had been up so long.

The two railroad tracks stretched themselves out in the sun and disappeared like a pair of silver strips in the distance. A freight car stood on the siding and I went up and looked at it. "Return to

Värtan" was written in chalk on its side. I compared myself to the railroad car; I had come here full of hope and now I would go empty, returning south over the banging rail joints. I walked around the car a couple of times but found nothing unusual about it. The station house slept in the sunshine, and an invisible clock ticked in a cabinet.

During those endless hours I saw the unfamiliar countryside awaken. Half-dressed, yawning, and fumbling with the front of his pants, a man came around a cabin corner or a woman went to the cellar to get cream for the morning coffee. Cows came out of the forests and their bells tinkled softly. They stood by the gates where the ground was worn and bellowed protractedly. A ramshackle cellar with milk bottles and a drowsy boy who gaped at the stranger.

Finally, off in the distance, I saw the rails disappear under the train. A middle-aged couple and their children were ready for a trip and the children's joy wakened a bleeding envy in my soul. The parents lined up the suitcases, blankets, and packages on the platform and then, with sullen and wondering eyes, tried to sort out who I might be. Their lives seemed to depend on managing to solve that mystery.

I saw most things around me all right and I turned in my ticket, like the others. On the train I drank tepid water from the carafe, but the tormenting red flame in my chest did not go out. At a larger station where the train made an hour's stop I drank two lagers for my sixty-two öre and dully hoped they would make me a little drunk and deaden my suffering. They cost thirty öre apiece and the waitress grabbed the two-öre tip with contempt.

It was evening again when I stepped off the train at home. I moistened my handkerchief in a stream and bathed my eyes before I went in, and when I looked at myself in my pocket mirror, I thought the past twenty-four hours hadn't marked up my mug too much. But Mother was of a different opinion.

"You look terrible," she said, horrified when I came in. But I was ready.

"Yes, I don't feel very well," I answered. "I drank water from a ditch and it probably wasn't too clean. I probably got a little poisoned from it."

"Oh, how could you let yourself do that? So much vermin floating around in such water. Was the young lady all right then?"

"Her, oh yes—she says hello, by the way."

"Such a long and expensive trip for nothing," Mother sighed. "And then coming home so miserable."

"I bet a lot of people have drunk from that ditch," Father said suddenly from behind his newspaper. "It probably isn't as unhealthy as it seems at first."

"You sure don't know that," Mother answered. "You've never set foot up there in Norrland."

"No, of course not, but it's a damned long old ditch. It shoots out a little everywhere."

I began describing the ditch anxiously; thus and thus it lay in relation to the road and there was wheat on one side. Did Father sit there thinking I was lying?

"No, no," Father answered. "Wheat, you say. I've always heard and read that they're not much for growing wheat in Norrland."

"Ha, ha, what talk." What the books said I didn't give a damn about—I believed more in my own eyes.

"Yes, yes, of course," said my father.

The fourteen days' grace period I had been allowed to find means for Nils Josef Valdemar's upbringing went by quickly and I could do nothing for him. I tried to accustom myself to becoming a forced laborer and thought in cowardly moments that maybe I could even become a good one. I read the law, too, and it gave me a little glimmer of hope. It said they could take me only if I neglected to pay child support out of laziness and indifference. Who would be able to call me lazy and indifferent? I worked, of course, if I ever got anything to do.

My heart beat heavily and unevenly when I thought about the workhouse, and I wondered if it was from cowardice. I studied myself and decided that if it were a pure and noble death, I could give my life for, say, an old man from the poorhouse, but this disgusting possibility frightened me.

Just as anxiously and hopelessly as Jesus in Gethsemane, I prayed to be spared the cup soon to be placed before me. I wanted to go off to war or anyplace else where there was hope of being killed by another man.

The county deputy came one morning in his rickety gig. He tied his old jade to the gatepost and walked in without knocking on the door. His yellowish-gray hair hung in wisps around his head when he laid his pride and joy, the striped cap, on the table.

"Well, well," he said in a tone between self-importance and bantering, "now we're going to go out for a little ride, you and me. I bet you can guess where it's off to."

Then I turned cowardly and piteous like never before, and my stomach turned inside me.

"It's probably best that you change your clothes," the deputy continued. "Or are you going like that?"

Then I tried to escape like a scared child.

"I don't have any shoes," I said in a weak voice. "I have nothing but these clogs here." And I put out a clog.

"Oh, yeah," said the deputy and his shallow black eyes wandered about the room, troubled by the shoe problem. It was quiet a while and then I heard the coachman's housekeeper open her door and sneak up to ours to listen.

"But you've got to go—and today," the deputy said, looking around the corner into the kitchen for something I could put on my feet.

"Surely you can let him stay home," Mother said from the stove. "He's not well either."

"Yes, there's a lot wrong with him," Father agreed. "Besides the kid isn't his anyway."

"I'm just following orders," said the deputy contentedly, straightening his frame, which for fifty years had bent over plough and harrow. "But he can't go there without something on his feet, of course. Once he's there he'll get their shoes, but for the trip, you see."

"I only have these here anyway," I said.

"You can come along to the telephone," it dawned on the deputy. "I'll call and ask the county sheriff what I should do."

"Surely I can stay here; I'm not going to try to escape."

"Ha, ha, that's probably true, but you come along with me anyway."

The housekeeper trotted back in when she heard us coming, and when we walked by her window, her snout sat on the pane like a full moon. A wild delight gave it an impressive luster.

When the deputy saw the telephone, his rugged face took on a respectful expression. He bowed to the receiver when he heard the sheriff's voice.

"Yes, well, I've got the Hård boy here," he said, "but I don't know what I should do. He has no shoes, you see."

"He has to have some shoes, damn it," screamed an angry tin voice from the receiver.

"He only has clogs he says and . . . ."

"Well, so take him in his clogs then," screamed the thick-stomached helper of Justice, and the deputy trembled as he hung up the receiver.

"The boss was angry today," he whispered. "He was probably out drinking last night. Then he's always in a bad humor the next day."

Through a gantlet of curious and malicious looks we came back to our cabin, and I hopelessly brought out my worn-out shoes. When I put one on, the deputy took the other in his hand and examined it.

"You'll go far in these here, ha, ha," he said, trying to encourage me. "I don't have much better myself."

Father and Mother tried to save me with various objections. What did they want with me at Svartsjö? I wasn't fit for heavy work and never would be, sickly as I had been lately.

"But who can show that I'm lazy and indifferent?" I asked. "Sure, I'll work if I can just find something to do."

"They say your work isn't worth much. You walk around staring into the forest instead of working. Your last employer has vouched for that," said the deputy.

When I was ready, I couldn't take my parents by the hand and say good-by like when you're taking a trip. I knew I was going away for a year; the law book said so.

"Yes, well, good-by then," I said to them from the door without looking at them. I heard Mother run into the bedroom and Father clear his throat as if he were thinking about saying something.

The coachman and his housekeeper stood in the yard. She held her hands under her apron on her enormous stomach. Both the old people grinned horribly when the deputy came out with me.

"What did I tell you?" the coachman asked with a toothless grin. "Wasn't I right?"

"That's tit for tat," the housekeeper observed contentedly.

I didn't answer but walked up to the old gig. The horse laid his annoyed ears back and bit into the gatepost when I climbed up.

Everywhere in the fields people straightened up and followed us with their eyes. I sank down as much as I could so no one would recognize me, but the deputy turned proudly to all sides to see if they noticed his cap. On a box behind the seat sat one of his boys, who would drive the gig home from the station.

On the train the deputy wanted people to think he was out with a dangerous criminal. He watched me constantly with his washed-out eyes and answered shortly and condescendingly if I said anything. When I walked out on the platform, he followed along with a rigid expression on his face as if he wished to say, "This one is extremely dangerous, this one here, good people, but stay calm; I'm the man to handle him."

Towards noon he took out some large slices of bread and munched on them. I saw from the side how hard his jaw worked; a big bone moved up and down when he chewed. "In a few years," I thought to the bone, "you will stop for all time, no matter how fussily your owner moves you now to keep up his body and to manage his job officiously and haughtily." I admired the society that understands so well how to use its obedient small parts and persecute its disobedient parts to their last movement.

Because the deputy's post and demeanor made him my enemy, I

started to hope all possible harm should come to him. I sat thinking about what should happen. He had been a widower for many
years, but when he was chosen deputy, he put on his cap and pro-
posed to a younger woman. She looked at his cap, thought about
the farm he owned, and said yes. Now he was married to her
and she most likely had buttered the slices of bread he had just
chewed up.

Naturally, she's unfaithful to him, I thought. She's waiting for
him to kick the bucket so she can get herself a younger man. She'll
come along with the people in the funeral procession, looking
around for another man while she dries her eyes with her handkerchief. And you'll lie there with your cheekbones motionless
even though you're a county deputy, and someone else will march
around with your dear striped cap on. So I thought, feeling spiteful even though the deputy was only doing his duty by taking
me in.

But now he was alive and had the upper hand. He was just that
zealous for the whole trip, even when we had stepped off the train
and went plodding on foot towards the big building ready to de-
vour me. We walked in through a big iron gate and past some old
men who were moving dirt. They stared dully at us, all of them
with matted beards. I did not see one my own age. The guard by
the gate showed us into a little room with a table and a bench. Just
afterwards, a man with a blue suit and commanding face came in.

"Good day, deputy," he said, taking first the deputy and then
me by the hand. "Are you here with another old inmate?"

"Yes, but not exactly old," said the deputy, somewhat disappointed at the superintendent's mistake.

"Oh," said the gentleman, stiffening. He was angered that he
had greeted me, believing I was a friend of the deputy's. "Are the
papers on him ready?"

"Oh, yes." The deputy groped in his pocket and took out the
consignment notes on me. The superintendent glanced through
them and pushed a button. A guard came in and stopped by
the door.

"There's an empty bed in number six, isn't there?" the superintendent asked.

"Yes."

"Put this one here in it. Then he can check out some clothes so he can get in on the dirt removal tomorrow morning."

I thought of telling about my bad heart, protesting that I could not manage heavy work, but the prisoner's usual cowardice gripped me and I was silent. I turned around at the door and looked at the deputy, but he misunderstood me completely in his haughtiness.

"Oh, yes, I'll say hello to your parents," he said condescendingly. "Good-by."

The pensioners had had their evening porridge and lain down on their beds before I came in. There were five of them and I was the sixth.

"There's your bed," said the guard, pointing towards a corner. "You'll be in it at nine o'clock. You can't have any food tonight."

"Well, that's sure a damned thing," said a bass voice from behind a newspaper. "Can't he eat? Maybe he hasn't had a bite all day."

The other four agreed, mumbling. But I, who wanted everyone to think me hardened and unmoved, I answered that I didn't give a damn about their food. The five old men let their newspapers drop and looked at me as I said that, sitting down on my bed.

"What do they have you in for then, boy?" one of them asked, one with a red nose between a pair of large, white moustaches. He looked at me with gentle blue eyes when he talked. The guard had gone out.

"I was sentenced to pay for a brat that isn't even mine and when I couldn't do it, I had to come here."

A couple of the old men cackled behind their newspapers.

"Yes, of course you're innocent, damn it. It's the same way with the rest of us—we're innocent too. We'd want to support both our old women and brats if we could," said a squeaking voice.

I didn't answer but looked around in the barracks. By the window stood a table with numberless scratches and dents in it. An ink bottle and a letter lay on the table. On the letter lay fifteen öre for a stamp, and when I had stared for a moment I could read the address: Mrs. Josefina Svensson, 7 Gåsgränd. Later I saw her one day when she came to visit her husband. She was tall and stern, with warts on her chin, and I realized why Svensson got along so well at the facility.

After the old men got to know my name, what I did, and whether I had slept with any girls the night before, they were quiet. After a while, I asked if they thought I could go out and look around. Now, while I had my clothes on.

"Well, you can ask the head guard," said the gentle voice from the white moustache. "He's human so it might work."

The head guard looked at me a moment as if my request had been absurd or at least unusual; then he got up and pointed to a place where I could walk. It could be seen from his window. Yes, I could walk a while; he thought he knew I was a decent boy so he didn't need to worry about any stupidities from me. But at nine the signal goes off, and then everyone has to be in bed.

The sun was still up, the same sun as at home, I thought, starting off on the designated road. It was beautiful here, too, although society's refuse was collected here. Maybe just one in ten thousand is in for forced labor, I thought, and I'm that one. And still I've read philosophy, prayed to an unknown God, and always striven to become something more than ordinary. Now I was walking here; my young, tall body would walk for a year among the old men ruined by alcohol. As long as I didn't die of a heart attack during the year. I couldn't manage moving dirt and stones.

The sunshine lay evening-yellow on the bushes by the road, the air stood as still as a glass cover, and there was a delicate pre-autumn feeling round about me. A dry juniper shrub thrust up like a flame out of the ground a little way from the road.

Yes, now I belonged to the lowest of those numerous groups you could divide six million people [1] into. A murderer stands higher in esteem; he enjoys a certain reputation for his having given people a sadistic experience. But who cares about a forced

1. The population of Sweden at the time the novel takes place.

laborer, a negligent of society who doesn't even get into the newspapers?

Father and Mother didn't have it so good either with an off-spring like their son Lars. Lucky the other children were ordinary folks who worked with their hands, got married, and had children, invited each other for coffee and backbit each other harshly. Occasionally they even paid their taxes and sent home apron material for Mother's Day. The old saying about the rotten apple could surely comfort the parental heart a bit, too.

A long-billed bird suddenly lit in a tree a little way from the road. It was black and white, with a long beak, and I thought it was a sea bird since the sea wasn't too far away. It looked around, opened its long bill, and emitted a complaining, two-toned cry.

"God damn," I thought the bird cried. Becoming interested, I forgot my great misery for a moment. Was it the facility's black soul that had taken form to bewail its evil fate, a flying digest of the huge, white-plastered hell? I liked the thought and built more upon it. The bird had to be the product of the prisoners' collective suffering flying around, grumbling its distress over the emptiness of the universe. Turning round and looking at the facility, I noticed a man walking a little way behind me. When I turned, he stopped, taking interest in the sunset.

It was a guard, all right, who would take me if I should run away. They didn't more than half believe me—but then how could they know that I didn't have the courage to escape? Before the deputy took me, I thought no power in the world would be able to hold me prisoner; over walls and past guards I would walk irresistibly to freedom. That's how great the need for freedom was in me, and it was that great in all the more meaningful humans, I thought then. But now I saw that I deceived myself even in that respect. There was no revolt in me; the damn thing was only in my thoughts and mouth.

"God damn," cried the bird, flying to another tree. The prison guard was absorbed in the sunset with one eye, the other watching me. I saw his coarse body and moustache, his watchful posture, the whole of the well-trained machine, and again I admired the society that knows so well how to choose its servants. If I had been the prison guard and he the prisoner, I would have gone up and talked intimately—against regulations—with him. I would have talked about what the frost-bitten sedge in the ditch was called in Latin or what I thought about eternal life. If he had yearned for freedom, I would have helped him over the wall. That's right.

And if I had been one of the clerks behind the counter or window at the child welfare bureau and a clumsy, distressed, guilty or not-guilty, papa had come from the country, I would have shown him the way without contempt in my manner and bearing. I would have done that without boasting. And therefore I could not be used for anything very important. Society didn't give a damn if I knew everything about the Ice Age, the star Mira, and the flowers. Persecute and strangle the one who doesn't fit in but rather persists in living just as life rises up and whispers in him.

So I thought as the day's massive star sank in the west. I turned and walked back to the facility to take my place among the red-nosed, unshaven, poor wretches inside. The guard didn't look at me but turned and followed me back.

One of the youngest of the old men lay in the bed nearest mine. He had bushy eyebrows and a beard that showed traces of having once been red. His voice was deep and harsh.

He sat up in bed, fixed his eyes on me, and said, "Well, so now you're here."

"That's right, but maybe it won't be for long. I'm weak, and I can't do heavy work."

"If you've come here, you'll be here until the year is up. Everyone tries that stuff about being sick in the beginning, but it doesn't work. The doctor kicks them out straight off when they're examined."

"But I have a bad heart."

"So what? It's not against the rules here. Your shoulders are as broad as a barn door and you'll probably get to take on the stone cart tomorrow."

"What do you get per day for that then?"

"Are you stupid or just sitting there joking?"

"Joking? You must get paid something at least. They even get a little on Långholmen.[1] You have to be able to support the kid you're responsible for, you know."

"No, my boy, that's just the damnedest thing," said the red-bearded man, laughing contentedly. "Here you are to work for a year, and when you walk out you won't have earned one öre, but your debt to the child welfare bureau will have grown by several hundred."

"Jesus Christ! While they hold me prisoner here?"

"Oh, yes. It's punishment and training they're giving us here, so really we probably ought to be paying them, hee hee. They're well-meaning and want to make men of us. As for me, they thought of it a little too late, but you, a young boy, can surely come up to the surface again."

Up again, I thought. For sixteen years this will pursue me and then coming up won't mean a thing.

"It's the worst for the first few days, then you get used to it," the red-bearded man continued saying. "We old men thrown in here for drinking don't miss hardly anything else but booze. Otherwise, we had just as big a hell at home as here. It's worse for you boys who are used to having women. You're not married, are you?"

"No."

"Good thing—then you don't have to lie here thinking somebody else is taking care of your old lady for you at night. The last time I was here about two years ago . . . ."

"The last time? Is this the second time you've been here?"

"Third."

"But can they keep you more than one year here?"

"Hee, hee, one year at a time, you see. You can go free for a few days when the year is up, but then they'll take you in for a new year if they think they have some reason. But I wanted to talk about the guy in the bed next to mine two years ago. He was married and he didn't get his woman out of his thoughts night or day.

1. Långholmen, located on an island of the same name in the Stockholm area, was the largest prison in Sweden.

We weren't nice either but told stories about infidelity and such things until he went completely wild at night."

"Yes, that's not so easy," I said, thinking about the heavy road I had walked two weeks ago.

"No, you're right. But so one night he played with himself just like when you're with a woman. I woke up but he didn't even care that I was looking. Then I said, 'What are you doing? I'm going to tell the others about it in the morning. Good God.' But he swore and said he didn't give a damn. Afterwards, he said there wasn't a man or woman in the whole world who hadn't done the same as him some time. I said it wasn't right anyway and I would squeal to the others.

"'I pretend it's my wife I'm with,' he said then. 'I think it kind of makes the whole thing more all right.'

"You see, then you don't think it's right either," I said. Then he got mad.

"'Not right! Go to hell, you and your faggy red beard,' he said and turned towards the wall. I told the others the next day though there was probably no need. It didn't help anyway, since pretty soon he did it even though people were awake and it was almost light inside. So there's good reason for my saying it's worse for the young than for us old men."

"Surely you can get along without girls for a while," I answered, but the red-bearded man grinned in his beard.

"He said so too—during the days. But we know how well he got along."

The August night stood gray and silent outside the window. The old men breathed heavily and one of them snored. I was still a little surprised about everything around me; it hadn't quite dawned on me yet that I, Lars Hård, who always felt myself born for something special and above the others, sat here unable to go where I wanted. The old man right across from me took off his clothes and scratched his hairy legs while he peered thoughtfully at me. I saw he was thinking of saying something more, but I hoped he would be quiet.

I had met people everywhere who knew very well how my life ought to be arranged and lived. This old man was full of wisdom and good advice, too, but here he sat, a prisoner in his old age anyway, and Father would have likened him with pleasure to a fly shit in importance.

A while later, I ran backwards out of the way of all blows and all threats from the law and society; I ran backwards and held my sick heart out in my hand in defense. But finally great resignation came, enveloping everything in the cold mist of indifference. The flowers, the stars, and the books pulled away and disappeared in a gray row of heavy days and nights.

I pulled those few bright memories out and looked at them occasionally, just like a child pulling tinsel off a Christmas tree plundered on the twentieth day of Christmas and left lying out in the snow the day after. I noticed how more and more I came to be like the old men around me. At work and at night I laughed "ha ha" and "ho ho" at the coarse remarks and stupidity I had loathed before. I heard myself brag and surprised myself. Something dragged me down with great force even though I stretched my arms out towards heaven.

All this, in other words, has been two years of my, Lars Hård's, life, and I don't know what anything depends on or where the great fault lies. But I'm beginning to feel a kind of delight in dipping my soul into every pool I come to. If I didn't get to be the best human being, then I'll become the worst. Before my year is up, I'll think of a way to become the most extraordinary among all the poor wretches who in grim and uniformed company travel between the big stone buildings with the iron fences, lost in the law's, the bureaus', and the uniforms' terrible claw grip.